GIRLS

Praise for books by Lil Chase

'A warm and funny story about friendship,
family and growing up'

Guardian

'Hilarious and charming'

Julia Eccleshare

'Very funny . . . realistic and scarily relatable'

Wondrous Reads

'An entertaining story . . . relatable and sweet'

Bookbag

'Compelling . . . full of neat twists'

Chicklish.o.uk

Books by Lil Chase

Boys for Beginners

Secrets, Lies and Locker 62

The Boys' School Girls: Tara's Sister Trouble
The Boys' School Girls: Abby's Shadow
The Boys' School Girls: Obi's Secrets

Lil Chase
THE BOYS' School GIRLS

Obi's Secrets

Quercus

First published in Great Britain in 2015 by

Quercus Publishing Ltd
Carmelite House
50 Victoria Embankment
London EC4Y 0DZ

An Hachette UK company

A CIP catalogue record for this book is available
from the British Library

PB 9781782069843
EBOOK 9781848668195

10 9 8 7 6 5 4 3 2 1

Typeset in Perpetua by Nigel Hazle
Printed and bound in Great Britain by Clays Ltd, St Ives plc.

For Kate,
my best friend.

Chapter 1

It's the same thing as always when our class queues up for assembly.

'Quick! Come sit next to me.' Donna grabs Sonia and pulls her into the line.

The same sense of panic: I've got no one to sit next to.

Last year Hillcrest High was a boys-only school. We're the first girls they've allowed in and there are just ten of us. If you don't get a good place in the line for assembly, you end up sitting next to one of the boys. Yesterday I was next to George Daniels, and he picks his nose. The day before it was Mo Hussain and he's a gigantic bully. I'm not being the odd one out again today.

I barge into the middle of the row. 'Hannah,' I say, 'sit next to me.'

I wedge myself in between her and Abby before

Hannah gets her usual spot next to Indiana. And, of course Abby's next to Tara, her best friend.

Crisis averted. This time.

'Get yourselves together, Year 8,' Mrs Martin says. 'We have a special treat for you in assembly today.'

I groan. '*Special treat* is code for *something lame*,' I whisper to Hannah.

She rolls her eyes. 'Tell me about it.'

As we file into the hall, us ten girls in among all these boys, the music starts up. A violin squeaks as the bow passes over its strings, making me wince. A second violinist joins in and he's no better. Just as I'm thinking it couldn't get worse, the cello starts, completely out of time. Craig Hurst puts his hands over his ears – which is rude, but I can't blame him. I'm close to pulling my ears off.

Year 8 takes up four rows in the middle of the assembly hall, behind the Year 7s. If this is the special treat, it needs work. I'd do a much better job if I was up there with my trumpet. At least I think I would. Ever since Dad's shifts changed and Mum got her new job they've both been too

2

busy to drive me to lessons, so my brothers are the only people who have heard me play recently: Jumoke is ruder than Simon Cowell when I ask him for feedback – *It stinks worse than Dad's feet.* And Bem puts in his earphones.

Big brothers: can't live with them, can't get them adopted.

Hearing this classical piece now – even sounding so awful – makes me miss playing.

Lenny Fulton is sitting in the row in front of me, cringing. He must have felt my stare because he turns, sticks out his tongue and flops his head to the side like he's a corpse. I smile back at him.

Donna pulls a face like a corpse too, laughing afterwards. Sonia laughs along. Of course.

Donna thinks Lenny directed that look at her. Maybe he *did* and I'm the idiot for thinking he was looking at me. But then why is Donna throwing me an evil stare? Either way, I'm not getting involved. I turn to Abby and whisper, 'This is the background music they play in hell.'

She giggles behind her hand.

Finally it stops. The school claps politely.

'Thank you for that, boys,' says the

headmaster – Mr Macadam – as he stands up from his chair and adjusts his trousers over his belly. 'Can we have another round of applause for our very own string quartet?!'

We all clap again, a little more raucously. We're just relieved it's over.

Mr Macadam says good morning, then thanks everyone who helped out at the Winter Festival in Wimbledon Village this weekend.

Next to me, Abby shudders.

'. . . so lovely to see the fireworks and hear all those lovely carols being sung. It was a fabulous night,' he says.

I throw Abby a sympathetic look. What happened to her on that night was the opposite of fabulous – it was terrifying. She seems OK now . . . *ish*. But maybe that's only because Tara has grabbed her hand. They're best friends again. And because they are, Abby can handle anything.

'And on that note . . .' Mr Macadam bursts into a smile. '*Note*, get it?'

Everyone else groans, but I choke back a laugh. Bad jokes are better than no jokes at all.

'I want to talk to you about this year's

Christmas concert,' he continues. 'The orchestra have been practising for a week or so now.'

Orchestra? Why didn't I think of that before?! I could play with people who care about performance and I'd finally know what I sound like. Classical music isn't my thing, but it would be worth it to perform in a *group*. Not 'big band' exactly but a big group . . . which is close. Big band *is* my thing. And Mum and Dad wouldn't have to pick me up or drop me off so it shouldn't be a problem for them.

'Orchestra?' Hannah whispers beside me.

'I know!' I whisper back, excited. I wonder if Hannah wants to join too. What does she play?

'Lame,' she says.

I quickly hide my smile. 'It's not lame! It's . . .' But I trail off as I look along the row of girls. Tara's pulling some fluff out of Maxie's hair, while Candy examines her nails and Indiana fiddles with the tail end of her plait. They all think it's lame too. '. . . lamer than a fish on dry land with a pair of broken crutches,' I finish.

Hannah does a half-smile. 'No, that joke was

5

lamer than a fish on dry land with a pair of broken crutches,' she says.

I thought that was actually a pretty good joke.

'The school wanted to do something a bit special this year,' Mr Macadam continues, 'so we've brought in an expert.' He turns to the side of the stage and raises his arm. 'Allow me to introduce Miss Rotimi. She's a professional musician, music teacher and conductor.'

Mr Macadam waits for the school to give an *oooh* of appreciation, but none comes.

'Rotimi?' I whisper to Abby. 'That's a Nigerian name.'

Abby nods, but goes back to chewing the sleeve of her jumper. I'm half Nigerian, so I guess it's not a big deal to anyone but me.

Mr Macadam hurries on. 'She often gives private lessons at the school so you might have seen her around, but this year she has the honour of taking charge of the concert.'

Miss Rotimi walks out and, encouraged by Mr Macadam, everyone claps. She's very pretty, with dark skin and oval eyes. Her light blue wraparound dress is way too fashionable for a regular teacher, showing a bit of her thigh as she walks, but not enough that it's inappropriate. She wears her hair in a bun, with a sparkly hairband round the front of her head.

I'm going to try to do my hair like that tonight.

Just raising her lips to smile is enough to make the whole school quiet down and listen.

'Thank you, Mr Macadam,' she says, a slight Nigerian depth in her voice. 'Thank you, boys.' She catches sight of us girls. 'And girls!' she adds.

I smile, but the boys laugh like they were the funniest words ever spoken. I like a bad joke, but that wasn't even a joke. Just because she's pretty!

'The orchestra have been practising for a week or two now and we're making real progress with the numbers.' She looks around proudly, seeking out the members of the orchestra. 'Normally the Christmas concert is just an instrumental show, but I thought it would be nice to have some vocals in it this year.'

Abby leans over and whispers to me, 'I bet you-know-who is paying attention now,' she says.

We both look over at Donna. She's sitting

straight up and is staring intently at Miss Rotimi. Sonia is whispering to her, no doubt stroking her ego like she's a Persian cat.

'There are going to be two solo parts,' Miss Rotimi continues. 'One male, one female. Keep an eye on the music noticeboard because I'll be holding auditions soon.'

Donna gasps. She sits up even straighter. Sonia reaches over and squeezes her hand.

'Who knows the song *Baby, It's Cold Outside?*' she asks.

Donna is the first to throw her hand in the air. I raise my hand too. It's a good song, catchy and wintery and, most importantly, a big-band swing number with loads of brass, including trumpets. It's right up my street!

Everyone in the assembly hall starts muttering about it. Other people know the song as well.

Tara, seeing my hand in the air, asks me, 'Are you going to audition?'

Donna must have heard because she looks over. 'I don't mean to be rude, Obi,' she says, 'but I wouldn't waste your time. I'm going to go for it, so . . .'

I don't mean to be rude, Donna, I think to myself, but you haven't heard me sing.

But really I'm nowhere near as good as Donna. She sings with this band called Sucker Punch, and she's got an amazing voice.

'Nah,' I say. 'I sound like nails on a blackboard. Worse than the string quartet in fact.'

Donna seems satisfied, smiles and relaxes. Then she leans forward and says to Lenny. 'You should try out for the boy solo.'

Lenny pulls a face. 'I don't know, Donna,' he says. 'I'm more of a hang-at-the-back-of-the-stage-with-the-drummer kind of guy.'

'What are you talking about?!' Donna says, shoving him on the shoulder. 'You come forward to perform with me for that one song I wrote, *You, Me and She*. We harmonize perfectly.'

'I suppose . . .' he says.

'It makes sense if we both go onstage together for the Christmas concert.'

'It does,' Sonia butts in. 'You two already have the onstage chemistry!'

Candy giggles.

Donna ignores them, but I can tell she's trying not to smile.

Lenny's turned away to face the front and I can see Donna whispering to Sonia. 'I'll get him to sign up,' she says, and flips her hair.

Sonia nods. Of course she will.

Sometimes it's hard not to be jealous of Donna. She has Lenny – the best-looking boy in Hillcrest – and she's really pretty, and she has the voice too. She's got more gifts than Santa.

'Quieten down please, Hillcrest,' says Mr Macadam. 'I'm glad you're excited, but our guest hasn't finished her announcement.'

'Thanks, Mr Macadam,' says Miss Rotimi, 'but I sort of *am* finished.'

Mr Macadam blushes as he smiles at her. She's just made him look like a muppet and still he's got goo-goo eyes.

'I hope lots of you will audition,' she says. 'Oh, and it's not too late to join the orchestra too.'

I won't be auditioning to sing, but orchestra is tempting. Especially if they do swing numbers like It's Cold Outside. What about the girls? If they think orchestra is lame, would they think I was lame if I joined?

'Thank you, Miss Rotimi.' Mr Macadam smiles at her as she leaves the stage. He turns back to us and does the rest of assembly – a reading about honesty, news that the Year 12 football team are doing well in some tournament, and a couple of room changes for the day. But all I can think about is orchestra.

He finishes with a reminder. 'Don't forget: auditions soon, classes right now. Have a good day, everyone.'

The girls and I gather outside the hall. 'What have you got?' Hannah asks me.

I mentally check my timetable. 'English,' I say. Then I feel the panic suddenly rising again. 'Can I sit next to you?'

'Sorry,' she says. 'Candy already asked.'

It's like they book their seating plans weeks in advance.

'See you at break, yeah?' Maxie links arms with Indiana. They're in a different English class to me.

There's another girl, Simone. But she keeps

her distance from the rest of us girls – no idea why. If only she would talk to us, then our numbers would be even and I'd have someone to sit with. There's no point asking Tara and Abby, or Donna and Sonia – they always sit together because they're best friends.

I've never had a best friend. When we started Hillcrest, I thought I would find one. But with only nine girls to choose from, the odds are even lower. Maybe it's because I'm different to everyone else – liking things like orchestra, and swing music, when they're all into the normal, popular stuff that's on the radio. And I'm the only mixed-race girl in the school.

Why is everything here so complicated? I do want to be in a band. I want to play the music I love. But I'm tired of being by myself all the time. I want a best friend more.

Though I can't do anything about where I've come from, there are things I can do something about. I need to try to act normal.

Chapter 2

I run down the field, dribble past Bem and whack the ball. Jumoke doesn't get a hand to it and it slides in.

'Gooooaaaal,' I yell, and raise my arms as I lap the playground.

It's after school, and me and my brothers have come back to play some football. It's a cold night, but I've warmed up after running around for a bit, and the street lights from the road mean the playground isn't completely dark.

'Good shot, toad face!' Bem's way of congratulating me.

Jumoke sighs as he runs off to get the ball. 'Not fair,' he calls over his shoulder. 'I was put off by the noise.'

The noise *is* off-putting. Especially for me. I didn't realize orchestra would be practising tonight. I still want to sign up for it, but I don't want the girls to tease me.

Bem laughs. 'You just can't take being beaten by your twelve-year-old sister.'

I keep glancing across at the school building, trying to listen to what they're playing, wondering if I would fit in. *O Come, All Ye Faithful* could have used some more brass in the 'O come, let us adore' him bits. I can imagine me and my trumpet really—

My thoughts are interrupted by a teacher walking out of the school. 'Watch out,' I say to my brothers.

'Should we make a run for it?' Bem wonders.

It's a bit naughty of us to be here. I squint my eyes to see which teacher it is. It's the beautiful lady – Miss Rotimi – from this morning. She hasn't got her coat on and she's hugging herself to protect from the cold.

'Nah,' I say. 'It's only Miss Rotimi. She's not even a proper teach—' But when I turn around, my brothers have already picked up the ball and legged it.

So they remember the football but abandon their little sister. Nice.

'Hello!' Miss Rotimi calls out to me. 'No need to run off,' she adds, just in time, because I was seriously considering it.

'Er . . . sorry,' I say to her. 'We go to school here. Were we disturbing you?'

'Not as much as we were disturbing *you*, I imagine!' Miss Rotimi says with a chuckle. Her bright white teeth shine as she laughs. She's one of the most beautiful women I've ever seen in real life. I mean, my mum is beautiful – slim, with freckles over her cheeks and blonde hair. But with her Nigerian features Miss Rotimi is beautiful in a way that *I* might be one day. It's nice to think it's possible.

'We're not really supposed to be here,' I admit.

Miss Rotimi winks at me. 'What Mr Macadam doesn't know won't hurt him.'

She's so cool.

'I didn't mean to scare you away,' she says.

I shrug. 'My brothers are cowards.'

Miss Rotimi laughs again.

If she hasn't come to tell me off, what does she want?

'You're Obi, aren't you?' she asks.

How does she know *that*?

'Yes. How . . . ?'

Miss Rotimi taps her nose. 'A little bird,' she says, her eyes twinkling.

I scan my brain, trying to think of who would have mentioned me.

'The same little bird said you play the trumpet,' she adds.

I wrinkle my nose. 'How . . . ? Who . . . ?'

She taps her nose again. It's annoying, but I think she's trying to be friendly, so I smile. Maybe she knows my old trumpet teacher, Mrs Giwa, and she said something about me.

Miss Rotimi scrunches up her face. 'We really need a trumpeter in the orchestra . . .'

'I know. I heard,' I say.

Her face falls because I've just kind of insulted her orchestra. Me and my big mouth.

'I mean . . .' I say, trying to claw it back, 'it sounds good. But your brass section isn't as full as it could be.' I wish I could be the one to help fill it up. But I haven't had the chance to ask my parents about orchestra yet. They were arguing, then Jumoke asked if I wanted to play football. And I'm still worried the girls would take the mick if I joined.

'Come on,' she says. 'Please!' She tilts her head to the side and pouts.

Miss Rotimi isn't acting like normal teachers; she seems more like a kid.

'I'm out here in the cold actually begging you!' she says, shuffling her feet.

I laugh. She's very persuasive, but . . . 'I don't have my trumpet with me,' I say, pointing around the playground as if to prove that I didn't bring a musical instrument to play football.

'I have a cornet you can borrow,' she offers.

'Umm . . .' The cornet is supposed to be similar to a trumpet, but I've never even picked one up. It'd be great to be able to play more than one instrument. More strings to my bow – ha! Unless two times the instrument makes you twice as lame.

'Come on,' she says. She rubs her arms. 'Just join us for tonight. If you hate it, you don't have to come back.'

She must be pretty desperate if she's pleading

this hard with someone she's never even heard play. 'Well . . .' What's the worst that could happen? 'Oh, all right,' I say.

'Thank you!' Miss Rotimi claps her hands together. 'Now come inside before I freeze to death.'

She walks next to me towards the door, like we're friends. 'Do you think either of your brothers would like to join?'

'Jumoke plays trumpet too,' I tell her. 'But he's got GSCE work so I doubt Mum would let him.'

Miss Rotimi looks thoughtful. 'Hmm,' she says. 'I suppose that's understandable.'

'And you wouldn't want Bem and his bassoon. As you're a music teacher, I'm guessing you need to keep your hearing,' I joke.

Miss Rotimi laughs, which is kind of her. 'Thanks for the tip,' she says. 'Ah, well, as long as I have *you* here.' She puts her arm round my shoulder and gives it a squeeze. 'It'll be nice to have some female company.'

It's weird to walk with a teacher's arm around me, but luckily she drops it before we get inside the hall. The whole orchestra looks up. There are about thirty people, all boys. Now I understand why she wanted me here – it's intimidating. I'd kind of like her arm back for support. I feel myself blushing.

'Come on, gentlemen,' says Miss Rotimi. 'I told you to check through your music and make sure you have all the songs in the right order.'

Someone at the back of the hall catches my eye: Lenny Fulton. I can see him above everyone – not just because he's over six foot, but also because of his massively high quiff. I wonder how long he's been in orchestra.

He raises his left arm from his guitar strings and waves at me. I wave back.

I bet Donna doesn't know he's in orchestra as well as in Sucker Punch. Would she still want to be his girlfriend if she did?

Maybe he's not telling her about it, I think as Miss Rotimi hands me the cornet. Maybe he's come to the same conclusion as Miss Rotimi: what Donna doesn't know won't hurt her.

If Lenny's in orchestra, maybe orchestra isn't as lame as everyone thinks.

Chapter 3

Miss Rotimi puts down her baton and addresses the orchestra.

'That's all for tonight, guys,' she says. 'Keep practising, and I'll see you tomorrow.'

The sound of the music is still in my ears and it's making my head buzz. Dad says you learn music when you sleep. I never knew what he meant until now – I'm going to hear these sounds for hours, running over the notes in my head. Playing with other people has made me realize I need to worry less about what I'm doing and listen more to others around me.

When I turn my phone on, it instantly buzzes with a text. It's Mum:

Where did you three run off to? You're late for dinner! I hope you've finished your homework. I'll be checking when you get back.

I can hear the nagging tone through the text. I roll my eyes. Maybe if she and dad hadn't been so deep in *discussion*, we would have stuck around for a family meal.

Another text. This time it's Jumoke:

Want me to come and get u?

I'm still annoyed that they ran off and left me.

No, thanks — I've accepted a lift from a stranger. He's promised not to tie the ropes too tight.

Jumoke sends a smiley face. Then:

If you're sure?

I'm thinking about accepting after all, when I hear, 'Hi, Obi,' above me.

I look up. It's Lenny. He's carrying his guitar case. I don't say anything, just smile.

'Which way're you headed?' he asks.

'Past the High Street. Is your mum picking you up? Would she give me a lift?' I ask hopefully.

"Fraid not,' he says. 'But I could walk wi
you if you like.'

'That would be great, thanks,' I say. 'Let me
just text my brother.'

I reply to Jumoke:

I've got someone to walk home with me.

'Ready?' he asks me.

I nod and we start walking.

'So . . . orchestra?' I say to him.

He clenches his teeth and sucks in a big
breath. 'Miss Rotimi forced me.'

'I didn't think they had guitars in regular
orchestras,' I say.

'They don't!' he says. 'But Miss Rotimi said
she was desperate to boost numbers. I took
guitar lessons with her a while ago. She begged
me to come to at least one practice to see if I
like it.'

Exactly what she said to me.

'And?' I ask.

'Actually I had a lot of fun.'

'Me too.' It's nice not to have to lie to

someone about how much I like playing music. 'I've never played with other people before, always on my own – practising or in a lesson. And I've never used a cornet – I quite liked it.'

'Multi-talented, you,' Lenny says.

'I have no idea whether I'm *any*-talented, let alone multi-talented! Thing is, when I play on my own I never know how it sounds, not really. The only way I can tell if I'm any good is if I play *with* people. That way I know if I'm keeping up and if it sounds OK and . . .' I realize I'm totally rambling, drowning in my music obsession for a second.

'Don't doubt yourself,' he says. 'You were great.'

'Whatever!' I shake my head at him. 'There's no way you heard me from the string section.'

'I heard . . .' He looks down his nose at me. 'And you only fluffed maybe two-thirds of your notes.' He cracks up.

I whack him on the arm. 'Rude!'

'You know you're good,' he says.

'Do I?'

'Come on,' he says, tilting his head to one side. 'What does your instinct say?'

I frown. 'I always have to listen to so many other people, my instinct never gets a look in.' Maybe it's time I started tuning into it.

'It's what Granny Fulton always said to me.'

'She sounds very wise,' I tell him.

'Nuttier than a Snickers,' he replies. 'Except for that one saying.'

I laugh. I'm not intimidated by boys like some of the other girls are. I guess that's the one and only perk of growing up with two brothers. Most aren't worth bothering with, but some . . .

Lenny and I talk about music and football and stuff on TV and it's really nice. No pressure. He doesn't ask me about my feelings or which nail polish I prefer, which is great, because I hate those conversations. I don't have a favourite nail polish; the only time I ever tried to apply it, I got it all over the bed sheets and Mum totally flipped. And as for my feelings . . . I find them so complicated that I can't deal with them myself, let alone express them to other people.

We've already reached the Starbucks opposite the station and I hardly even noticed.

'Want to get a coffee?'

Suddenly the easiness has dropped. Two seconds ago I was relaxed, and now we're having coffee. What if we run out of things to say to each other? Lenny's Donna's boyfriend – what if people get the wrong idea and think I'm trying to steal him?

'You're paying though, yeah?' he adds with a cheeky grin.

And with that, I know it can only be a friend thing.

'Whatever,' I say. And I push the door into the coffee shop. 'You buy the coffee. I'll pay for the free napkins.'

He wrinkles his nose. 'Halves?'

'Deal.'

I order a hot chocolate with cream and he orders a latte. While he's getting sugar I find a table. Lenny puts his mug down, then takes the seat next to me. I take a sip of my hot chocolate, but it's too hot and I spit it out. 'That was classy!'

'Very!' he says with a laugh. 'So you aren't as perfect as you seem.'

What a weirdo. 'I'm nowhere near perfect,' I tell him.

His phone beeps and I carry on speaking as he gets it out of his pocket and checks it.

'You should see the state of my bedroom floor,' I say.

'You have a bedroom floor?' he asks, looking at the screen on his phone. 'I think I used to have one, but I haven't seen it in years.' He doesn't respond to the text, just puts his phone on the table.

'Me neither,' I say with a chuckle. 'Beneath the jungle of school stuff and the mountains of clothes, somewhere there's a path to my bed . . . so legend has it.'

'I didn't know you were one of those girls who was into clothes,' he says.

I'm not sure how to take that. 'Are you saying I've got no dress sense?' I reply, trying to laugh it off.

'No . . . I . . . er . . .' He shakes his head,

like he feels stupid for what he's just said. 'No, you look lovely. Always.'

Even though I know he's not being serious I can feel myself blushing. I try to hide it by draping a napkin over my head and batting my eyelashes at him. 'A contender for *Next Top Model*.'

We laugh and then both go quiet. Another one of my bad jokes. But the silence doesn't feel awkward.

'You've got brothers at Hillcrest, haven't you?' Lenny asks after a bit. 'Bem and . . .

'Bem and Jumoke,' I tell him. 'Jumoke is in Year 10. Bem's in Year 9.'

'Is that it?' he asks me. 'Just you three?'

'Two brothers is more than enough!' I say. 'They're all right, as brothers go, I suppose. Jumoke likes to act all tough, as the big brother. And Bem and I let him because it's easier that way.'

Lenny nods with his eyes half closed like he gets it. 'My sister's the same.' He pulls a chain out from under his collar. It has a purple guitar pick on it and he fiddles with it as he talks.

'She's always bossing me around. She's worse than my mum!'

I nod like I get it too. But the truth is, at the moment, there's not much that could be worse than *my* mum. Dad says we have to be more understanding, because she's really stressed by this big project at work. But lately she's a massive grump.

'And do either of your brothers, you know . . .' Lenny leans over and whispers in my ear, 'play an instrument?'

I love that we have to hide our love of music together. It's like our shared secret.

'I would tell you,' I whisper back, 'but then I'd have to kill you.'

He laughs.

'My dad used to play trumpet in a jazz band. He forced us all to do music,' I admit. 'We resisted at first, when he made us do lessons after school and practise every night. But now I'm glad he did. It's like part of me. Like my lungs or my heart. I couldn't live without it.'

I look at Lenny, feeling a bit embarrassed

28

about opening up like that. But he's nodding again. He understands.

'Is that why you came to orchestra?'

I shake my head. 'I was only at school because we were having a kick-about in the playground.'

'I didn't know you played football,' he says.

'Two older brothers.' I shrug. 'It's kind of mandatory.'

He looks around as if checking for spies. 'One older sister means I can plait hair. You tell anyone *that* and I'd have to kill *you*.'

This phrase has now become our thing. I don't think I've ever had a thing with anyone before.

'Do you think you'll go again?'

'I want to . . . and . . . well . . . if we're telling secrets . . .' I search my instincts for the first time. They seem to be saying that I can trust Lenny. But can I trust my instincts? 'I love big-band swing music – I know it's not cool.' I dare to look at Lenny and he's still listening to me. He doesn't seem to judge me so I continue. 'I'd do anything to play in a big band. And if it has to be in our lame school orchestra, then OK.'

I realize I've closed my eyes and got all

intense, imagining being onstage playing with a big band for real, so I try to pull some dignity back by changing the subject.

'But Mum can be quite strict about after-school stuff,' I tell him. 'Hopefully my dad will be able to talk her round.'

He nods slowly.

'I don't think the girls will understand,' I tell him, 'but it'd be worth being a social outcast if I get to play.'

I laugh, but Lenny doesn't join in. He looks thoughtful.

'Are you going back?' I ask him.

He shakes his head. 'I'm not as strong as you. I don't think I could take the teasing.'

It's weird to see a boy like Lenny show weakness.

'I should go after what I want,' I think out loud, 'no matter what anyone else says.' But then I remember everyone's else's reaction to the idea of orchestra. 'Hopefully no one will find out anyway. Do you think that's possible? If none of our friends come to the Christmas show, then maybe . . .'

His phone beeps again. He ignores it again. 'Who's that?' I ask.

He shakes his head. 'No one.' He looks annoyed with whoever's texting him.

'Your mum?' I guess, because my mum's texts are the most annoying texts in the world.

He shakes his head again. 'It doesn't matter,' he says quickly.

The phone beeps again and this time I can't help myself. I lean forward to check his display.

Donna.

He's had three texts in five minutes. Which is more than I've had in the last five days . . . unless you count texts from family . . . which I don't. I realize I'm jealous of Lenny because someone wants to talk to him. Even though it's Donna, who I don't even like that much.

'Don't worry about it,' he says, gesturing at his phone. 'What were we saying?'

But I can't let it go. Lenny's invited me here and we're having coffee. He said he thinks I'm perfect. We chat really easily. He's unbelievably good-looking. But if Donna knew I was thinking all this stuff about her boyfriend, she'd hate me. Sonia would hate me. And they'd make all the other girls hate me too. Then I'd be even more of an outcast with even less people texting me.

'I don't mind if you message your girlfriend.' My voice catches a little as I say it.

Lenny takes a deep breath. 'Donna's not my girlfriend,' he says. But he doesn't seem to mind me thinking that she is.

I tilt my head to one side. 'Really?'

'Really,' he says with a nod. 'Honest.'

I smile, relieved. If they aren't boyfriend and girlfriend, then I'm not doing anything wrong by hanging out with him.

I take a sip of my hot chocolate. Right now it's perfect.

Chapter 4

'Did you do the homework?' Abby asks me next morning in RE.

As a subject I'm not that keen on RE. But it's one of my favourite classes because the desks are in rows of three, which means me, Tara and Abby can sit together. Also, Mrs Fitz is such a flake that even if she remembers to set homework, she usually doesn't remember to collect it in, and she's always really late getting to class. Five minutes has gone and she's still not here. We're leaning back on our chairs chatting.

'Nah,' I say. 'I was about to start looking at it, but then my brother dragged me away to . . .'

'To . . . ?' asks Tara.

To play football and then I got sucked into joining orchestra. You might know it as 'lame' orchestra, which is why I have to lie about it.

'. . . to . . . listen to something on Spotify,' I finish. 'Did you do anything last night?'

'Not much,' says Tara. 'Abby came over and we tried out some styles with her new haircut.'

I turn my face away from them. They don't say these things to hurt me, but it does anyway. They've had a couple of fallings-out recently but they've been best friends for so long that there's just an understanding – they're a pair; I'm not included. I'm not even allowed to be offended. And I'm not. I just wish *I* had a best friend to spend time with.

'What else?' Tara asks me. 'Apart from listening to your brother's music.'

'Not much,' I say. Should I tell them about Lenny? I feel closer to Tara and Abby than the rest of the girls – especially as I had to help them with their drama that happened recently. I kind of want to spill the coffee beans.

'Did you hear about Lenny and Donna?' Tara asks.

My head whips up involuntarily. 'No,' I say quickly, then try to calm myself down. 'What?'

'Apparently they went out on a date last night,' she says. 'They went to the cinema.'

I laugh, but neither of them picks up on it. I always suspected half of Donna's stories were exaggerations, but I didn't realize that they were barefaced lies!

'Do you think that means they're an official couple then?' Abby asks Tara.

Tara shrugs. 'Only one way to find out,' she says, and gets her phone from her bag. 'You know she'll have updated her relationship status if they are.'

'They're not,' I blurt. Now it's their turn to whip round and look at me. Me and my massive foot in my even massiver mouth. Luckily Donna isn't in this class, but Sonia's sitting just a few desks in front of us and she's like an extension of Donna – her own personal spy.

'She didn't go to the cinema with Lenny last night,' I say, lowering my voice.

'How do you know?' asks Tara.

'Umm . . .' I start pulling on the hair at the back of my neck. 'Because I was with him last night.'

'WHAT?!!!' they both scream at the top of their voices.

The whole classroom goes quiet and turns to look at us. I turn red.

Abby giggles at the sudden attention. But as soon as the boys in the class realize that a bomb hasn't dropped, they go back to what they were doing – trading cards and playing games on their phones.

'It wasn't a big deal or anything,' I tell them quickly, trying to calm them down. 'We just got a coffee.'

Tara and Abby lean in. 'You had coffee with Lenny?' Tara asks.

'Was it, like, a date?' Abby's eyes are so wide I think they might roll out of her head.

'No!' I protest in a hushed whisper. I wish I'd never said anything. I glance at Sonia, who is coming over, desperate to get the goss. I speed-talk my next sentence. 'We just bumped into each other.' I don't say where. 'So Lenny asked if I wanted to get a coffee and I did so we did. End of. Now shush.'

'Does he fancy you?' Tara asks.

'No!' I screech. Did Sonia hear that? I grind my teeth together and glare at Tara – Sonia's only about a metre away now. 'Now *shush*.'

Sonia's at our desk. She stands over me with her hands on her hips and a stern smile on her face. 'What's going on?'

'Nothing,' the three of us say at the exact same time. Which doesn't lessen Sonia's curiosity.

'It's nothing,' I say. 'Honestly.' There's desperation in my voice.

Sonia cocks her head to one side. She's not that stupid.

Tara steps in. 'We were just talking about Donna and Lenny.' She's got a wicked smirk on her face, but I don't think Sonia's picked up on it. 'Did they meet up last night?'

Sonia's face goes from curious to smug, so happy that *she's* the one with the gossip. 'Not that it's any of your business . . .' she says, loving making it our business, 'but yes.'

Tara has her lips pursed, trying hard not to laugh. 'Really?'

'Yeah. They went to the cinema,' she says.

Tara snorts. This is bad. 'Oh really? What did they see?'

Just then the classroom door opens. It's Mrs Fitz. Everyone groans and very slowly moves back to their desks.

'Morning, class.' She's carrying a pile of books and her hair is coming out in all directions. 'Quieten down please, and we'll start.'

'Obi,' comes a whisper from behind me. It's Sam Caporn. He has a folded piece of paper in his hand.

'I said, *quiet, please,*' Mrs Fitz says more sternly.

I reach back and take the note. I can't imagine what Sam Caporn could want to say to me. Tara and Abby are looking too.

'It's from Lenny,' Sam adds.

Tara and Abby gasp. Sonia stops and turns back to my desk, desperate to know what the note says. I feel my heart fluttering. I hate being the centre of attention like this.

'Sonia,' says Mrs Fitz, 'sit down *now.*'

Sonia opens her mouth to say something, then stops. She looks at me, frowning, demanding to know what the note says. But class has started so I couldn't tell her if I wanted to.

I open the note. Tara and Abby lean over me as I read it.

Meet me in music room 4 at lunch. L x

Abby gasps, then slaps her hand over her mouth, grinning.

I can see Sonia glaring at us.

'He definitely fancies you!' Tara whispers, in a voice that's just loud enough for everyone to hear.

Sonia's eyes go huge. She beckons to me with her fingers, asking me to pass her the note.

'Turn around, Sonia,' Mrs Fitz says, her voice more threatening this time. 'Open your books to page 178.'

Sonia sighs and turns around.

I can't deal with this. What does the note mean? Why does it have to mean anything?

Beside me, Abby squeaks like a mouse as she gets her books out. 'Wait till Donna finds out Lenny fancies you,' she whispers into her open book.

I have to stop Donna finding out. And, anyway, Lenny doesn't fancy me – there's just no way. I'm not special enough. But then there's the coffee, and the things he said, and this note. I don't know what to think. I like Lenny. I really enjoyed hanging out with him. But sooner or later I've got to answer the Big Question:

Do I fancy Lenny?

Chapter 5

I spent the whole of RE not concentrating on anything Mrs Fitz said, just thinking about Lenny.

As soon as the bell went, Tara, Abby and me literally ran out of the classroom so Sonia couldn't follow us. We went to the girls' loos in the basement – the ones we never usually use – so she wouldn't find us. Tara insisted on making me put on lipgloss before I saw him.

And now I'm on my own, standing outside music room 4, and my pulse is racing like mad. Perhaps it's just from the excitement of running away from Sonia. I'm still not sure how I feel. I know I like Lenny, but do I *like* like him?

I take a deep breath. I really hope this isn't the moment when he declares his undying love for me. I wouldn't know what to say – I don't

want to lead him on and say I like him, but I
don't want to hurt his feelings and say I don't.
Because I'm just not sure. I try to listen to my
instincts, but they're being drowned out by the
thumping of my heart.

I mentally kick myself in the shin, just like
Bem does whenever he wants me to stop messing
around. *Get real, Obi!* I tell myself. There's no
way a cute guy like Lenny would fancy someone
like me.

I knock on the door.

I wait.

'Come in,' calls a voice from inside.

I take another deep breath and push the door
open.

Lenny's there, all alone. He's bent over an
amp and fiddling with some dials.

'Hi, Lenny,' I say. 'How are you?' My voice
is all squeaky and weird.

He doesn't look up as he says, 'Oh good, you
got my note.'

I nod quickly. 'Hmm,' is all I can manage.

'Thanks for coming,' he says, finally
straightening up. 'We have band practice in a

few minutes, but I want to ask you something before the others arrive.'

I close my eyes for a minute and then open them slowly. Should I tell him I don't fancy him before he humiliates himself?

'I was thinking . . . after I saw you last night . . .'

'And we stopped to get coffee on our way home because we were both thirsty,' I say, trying to make it clear that I don't think last night was a date.

'And we stopped to get coffee . . .' he repeats, raising his eyebrow like he's talking to a basket case. 'I was thinking about what you said about going after the things you want, no matter what other people say.'

'I was talking about orchestra,' I remind him hurriedly.

Just then the door pushes open. It's Reece and Joel and Donna. Now Lenny won't be able to ask me out. I don't know if I'm annoyed or relieved.

'Hi, guys,' I say to them through a clenched smile.

'Hi, Obi,' says Joel, taking a bite of a pasty and wiping his hands on his shirt. 'What are you doing here?'

Donna won't move from the doorway. She looks scared – her eyes are wide, looking from me to Lenny and back again. I smile at her, trying to let her know that we haven't just been snogging each other's faces off or anything.

'Yeah,' she says, 'what *are* you doing here?'

Lenny steps in front of me, as if trying to protect me from a pack of dogs. 'Umm . . .' he says. 'I was hoping to ask Obi before speaking to the rest of you, but . . .'

A rush of running feet comes racing up behind Donna. Then there's panting. Sonia slams into the back of Donna and peers over her shoulder into the music room. 'There you are.' She scowls. 'What are you doing here?'

The boys laugh.

'Poor Obi,' says Reece. 'That's the third time she's been asked that question in the last ten seconds.'

I force a laugh. 'Yeah, who do you think I am? Siri?'

No one's laughing with me.

Lenny says, 'Umm,' again, and all eyes, including mine, turn to him. This is it. He's about to ask me out in front of everyone. At least if he does it now Donna won't be able to kill me right this second. But I know she'll track me down later.

'So, well,' Lenny starts, 'I was thinking it would be cool if . . .'

'Spit it out,' Reece says.

'I reckon that Obi should join Sucker Punch,' he finishes.

The band look at each other in silence.

Meanwhile I exhale a massive breath. The first thing I feel is relief. I'd have been the centre of the goss for days if he'd asked me out in front of his band and I'd said *no*, or *yes*, or *I'm not sure* or *Can you ask me again later?*

'Obi?!' Donna spits. She looks at me. 'Not as a singer?!'

'*Definitely* not as a singer,' I reassure her.

But she doesn't look reassured.

My second reaction is disappointment. I've never been one of those special girls, never been someone people notice — not like Donna or Tara or Miss Rotimi. If Lenny had asked me out, then at least I'd know I'm fanciable.

I realize they're all waiting for some kind of explanation from me. Sonia is scowling the hardest. You have to hand it to her — she's a loyal friend to Donna.

'Obi plays trumpet,' Lenny tells them, 'and she wants to be in a band.'

Of course! What an idiot I am. *That's* what Lenny was talking about just now: going after what you want. This way I can be in a band and not get teased. Lenny is a genius and I could kiss him right now.

As a friend, of course.

Reece and Joel look at each other, clearly weighing up if a trumpet would be a good addition to the Sucker Punch sound.

Donna just looks confused. 'You never said you played the trumpet.'

'You never asked,' I reply. I don't mean to be cheeky, but Donna always wants everyone to know every detail of her life, but she never asks anyone about anything in theirs.

'I reckon a few of our songs would work well with a trumpety, brassy sound,' Lenny says.

Donna shakes her head frantically. 'No,' she says. 'It would drown out the vocals.'

'Nah,' he says, 'as long as the trumpeter uses a mute you can hear just fine.'

That told Donna.

'It'll give us a big-band influence,' he adds. 'Kind of jazzy.'

Lenny's remembered everything I told him last night. And he doesn't think I'm weird or lame. He wants to include me.

'You play big-band stuff?' Donna asks me, leering a little.

I feel a little embarrassed but I nod. 'I do. I love it. My dad got me into it when I was little,' I say apologetically.

Reece and Joel are eyeing me as if a love of big band is something to be suspicious of.

'A brassy sound might work with some of our faster songs,' says Reece, clearly thinking aloud.

'And actually,' says Joel, '*Call of Emotion* would sound pretty cool with a slow trumpet.'

'I don't know,' Donna cuts in. '*Call of Emotion* hangs off my voice. I don't know if we should corrupt it by adding a heavy trumpet sound.'

I roll my eyes. Corrupting the sound has nothing to do with it – she doesn't want me to corrupt Lenny.

Lenny cringes. 'Sorry, Obi, I should have talked it over with you first, but I should have talked it over with them first too. Looks like we're going to have to think about it.'

'We don't even know if she's any good,' says Donna.

'She is!' Lenny says. 'I've heard her.'

'When?' asks Donna, and from the way her voice cracks there's more to this question than just music.

'Last night,' he says.

Donna and Sonia shoot me the same look. *What happened when you were with Lenny last night?* Then Sonia's look changes as she remembers that Donna said *she* was with Lenny last night.

'Helloooo . . .' I wave. 'I am here, you know.' I turn around and head for the door. 'But maybe I don't want to be. I'll see you later.'

Reece's mouth is gaping and Joel's eyes are wider than a couple of bass drums. Lenny screws up his face. He looks really disappointed as I walk out and slam the door. But Donna's beaming. She couldn't be more pleased to see me go.

As for me, I don't know what to think. It's too complicated. If I could have my feelings surgically removed, I would.

Chapter 6

I'm still walking down the corridor, away from
the band practice that never was, trying not to
think about the looks on their faces as I stormed
off.

I walked into that room dreading the thought
of Lenny asking me out. Then when he didn't
I was hurt. Playing in a band is all I've ever
wanted. And even if Sucker Punch is not quite
big enough to be called big band, it's still small
band, which is better than no band. And being
in Sucker Punch would be easier than being in
orchestra because no one would tease me for it.
And I'd get to hang out with Lenny more.

But that would annoy Donna. And if I
annoy Donna, I annoy Sonia. And maybe they'd
convince the rest of the girls to be annoyed with
me and I won't have any friends. But if I join
orchestra they'll all think I'm lame and I'd risk

losing my friends anyway.

The more I think about it, the more confused I get.

'Hey!' comes a call from behind me.

I turn around. It's Donna and Sonia and I scowl at them.

'What?' I snap. 'I don't want to be in your stupid band so leave me alone.'

'What's going on with you and Lenny?' Sonia asks.

I'm so not in the mood for the third degree from Donna's henchman.

'What's it got to do with you?' I say.

'A lot,' she says, her hands on her hips. 'Lenny is Donna's boyfriend and Donna's my best friend and you're keeping secrets.' She narrows her eyes. 'Are you trying to steal him away from her?'

I look at Donna, her head held high. She's left her own band practice to come and confront me.

Sonia seems so sure they're going out. Donna seems so sure they're going out. Even though I know Donna's lying about last night, she was certainly texting him a lot. There is a chance that Lenny lied to me about them *not* being together.

But being accused of something I haven't done makes me want to kick a wall.

'You're right about one thing, Sonia,' I tell her.

Donna's eyes go wide and Sonia glances at her with concern as they both wait to hear my confession.

'I *am* keeping secrets,' I say. 'And I plan to keep it that way.'

I turn from them, but Donna puts a hand on my shoulder and spins me round.

'Umm . . . when did he hear you play? Last night, wasn't it? What were you doing together?'

'I don't have to tell you anything,' I say.

'Yes, you do,' says Sonia, stepping forward so she's right next to Donna. 'It's the Girl Code.'

'What's the Girl Code?' I ask.

Sonia's mouth drops open like I've just asked her what the alphabet is. 'Are you serious?'

I shrug. This is just another one of the million ways I'm different to everyone else. I must have been off sick when they were teaching the Girl Code.

'The Girl Code is about not keeping secrets from your friends,' Sonia informs me. 'It's about loyalty. Donna likes Lenny, and Lenny likes Donna, so it's your duty, as her friend, to keep them together.'

Hmm. We're all Boys' School Girls, and we said we'd always stick together, so I guess that means we *are* friends. But with Donna it doesn't always feel that way.

'Which means,' Sonia hasn't finished yet; she's jutting her head forward to make sure I'm listening, 'you have to tell Donna whenever you see him, and report back everything he says.'

'Really?' I ask. That sounds a bit crazy.

'Donna would do the same for you,' says Sonia, 'whenever you get together with a boy. Wouldn't you, Donna?'

Donna nods frantically.

I'm not sure Donna *would* do that if the situation was reversed. But it sounds like if I want to stay in with the first group of friends I've ever had, and the only girls in this school, I have to obey this Girl Code and spy on Lenny.

'So, where did you see Lenny?' asks Donna.

I get the idea of being loyal and helpful to your friends, but it's Lenny's secret that he was at orchestra. It's not a big one, but it's not mine to tell. I kind of want to see Donna's face when I tell her I had coffee with him last night so she knows I know they didn't go to the cinema. But I've only just learned about the Girl Code, and I don't think catching Donna out in her lie is part of it.

I sigh. 'We bumped into each other and went and had coffee and he heard me play.' Not lying, but I left out some parts.

'You can't have gone for coffee with him — ' Sonia crosses her arms in front of her chest — 'because Donna and Lenny went . . .' Sonia looks at Donna, who won't look back at her. Sonia frowns at the floor, trying to work all this out.

'Listen,' Donna says, and there is a definite threatening tone to her voice, 'next time you see Lenny out of school let me know, yeah?'

'What? *Every* time I bump into him?'

'Yes,' says Donna, as if her request isn't at all stalkerish. 'And if you do ever end up alone together – for whatever reason – would you ask him what he thinks about me?'

'If he's your boyfriend, don't you know what he thinks about you?' I ask.

Donna purses her lips and shakes her head.

Wow. Donna's always saying how she can control Lenny with just a flip of her hair. This is the first time she's admitted she might not be fully on top of the situation.

'*Is* he your boyfriend?' I ask. But I can hear my instinct, and it's telling me there's no way they're together.

She bites her lip. 'Umm . . . not officially,' she says. 'I thought we were because we speak loads and we hang out sometimes.'

My instinct was right.

'So did you go to the cinema?' I'm taking a risk, calling her on her lie – but I can't let her think I'm stupid.

Sonia's looking at Donna the same way I am – she's waiting for an explanation. I guess it's got to be rubbish for Sonia, finding out all the rumours you helped spread weren't true.

Donna laughs like this is all a silly misunderstanding. 'I met up with him on *Saturday*. We were supposed to go to the cinema, but then we couldn't be bothered.' She pulls her hair into a ponytail. 'I don't know where anyone got last night from.'

I can see Sonia's eyes wavering from side to side – just the way she looks when Mr Raza asks her a question and she has no idea what the answer is. 'You definitely told me you went to the cinema,' she insists.

Donna scrunches up her face. 'No, I didn't.'

I'm wondering if she's lying again, but then she gets her phone and shows us some pictures. There's a massive close-up selfie where she and Lenny are kissing her Yorkshire terrier. If it wasn't for the ten centimetres of dog between them, Donna and Lenny would be kissing each other. The date on the photo says it was taken on Saturday – so that part was true.

'I thought we were together, but he's never officially asked me to be his girlfriend. Can I assume that I'm his girlfriend?'

She looks so desperate I feel less angry.

I shrug. 'Sorry, Donna,' I say. 'When it comes to boy stuff, I'm useless . . .'

Donna's face falls and she looks at her feet.

'Unless you want to know how badly their bedrooms stink. My brothers share a room and it's a suffocation zone.'

At least she smiles at that. 'I just wish there was some way I could know for sure,' she says.

'You *do* know for sure!' Sonia says, stroking Donna's arm. '*I* know for sure. It's the way he looks at you. The way he is around you. He's not like that with anyone else.'

That's something I've never seen . . . only heard . . . from Donna. Sonia's gushing can be a little too much sometimes.

Donna flinches and pushes Sonia off her. 'Shut up, Sonia.'

She's being harsh to Sonia, but I can tell she's really upset. She likes Lenny and doesn't know where she stands.

'So, if you find anything out from him,' says Donna, 'you'll tell me, right?'

'Sure,' I say.

But I'm anything but. Following the Girl Code is like walking through a country meadow – it might look nice, but you never know when you're going to tread in poo. I'm staying as far away from this drama as possible. No matter how much I want to be in Sucker Punch, this isn't worth it.

But I do want to be in a band. Playing in orchestra last night has only made me more determined. If I'm going to go after what I want, and it's either Sucker Punch or orchestra, I guess I'm joining orchestra. Who cares what anyone else thinks?

Chapter 7

I press the valves on my trumpet and raise the end to the sky, blasting out *When the Saints Go Marching In* at the top of my lungs. I know it by heart because it's one of the first songs I ever learned to play. But I make little riffs from the regular tune to give my own take on it. I can't even hear Bem's drum and bass, only my music. It calms my mind. Without it—

'Obi! Bem!'

There's Mum's voice, somehow managing to penetrate my zone of chill.

'Yeah?' I shout back.

'Give it a rest, will you? I'm trying to work!'

I drop my trumpet to my side. She has no idea that I need to play to help me de-stress. I have to explain how much I want it. I'm going to ask if I can join orchestra. Right now.

When I walk into the living room, Mum

and Dad are in front of some house-buying programme. Mum's on her laptop, tapping away like a deranged pianist, while Dad's squinting at the TV. Mum's still in her work suit, but Dad's already changed into his scruffy trackie bottoms with the hole in the crotch. He's really gross.

Dad sees me, smiles, lifts the remote and turns the TV off.

'I was watching that!' Mum says, scowling at him. Then she sees me. 'Oh, sorry, darling,' she says to me. 'Sorry . . . darling,' she mutters to Dad, stumbling over the word.

'Are you all right, Obi?' Dad asks.

I get straight to it before something kicks off another argument. 'You'll never guess what.'

They both give me their full attention, their eyes full of hope.

'There is a Christmas concert at school,' I tell them.

'Hmm . . .' says Mum.

'What kind of concert?' asks Dad.

'With the orchestra. They've brought in a special teacher to run it and everything. It's like a big-band-type thing. And you know how much I like big band.'

Dad beams. He knows *exactly* how much I like big band.

'That's nice,' says Mum. But when I look over, her eyes have drifted back to her laptop again.

'Anyway . . . *Mum*,' I say. She snaps her head up and smiles at me, embarrassed. She knows she's been busted so she closes her laptop. 'I was thinking of joining.'

Dad jumps up from his place on the sofa. 'That's great!' he says. 'I was much older than you before I got into my first band.'

'It's not like a pop group or anything, Mum,' I tell her hurriedly. 'It's a school thing.'

Dad gazes at the photo on the wall of him blasting his trumpet. He looks so young and happy in it. 'That was taken during our world tour . . . all over Brixton!'

I giggle. 'Not sure that Brixton really counts as a world tour, Dad,' I say, 'but at least you had your fifteen minutes of fame . . . *ish.*'

'We were famous among those who cared

about *real* music,' he says. Then he puts one hand on his stomach and starts wiggling his hips in a circle. This is his version of dancing. To other people it looks like a symptom that needs physiotherapy.

'You keep your *real* music,' I tell him. 'This is going to be a normal music concert. All the favourite wintery hits with some swing numbers thrown in there. You know, stuff that people under the age of one hundred might like,' I joke.

'That's cheek for you,' he says. Then he starts muttering something in his Nigerian patois. I can't understand it, but I think I hear the words *big time.*

Oh dear, my dad is so deluded.

'We were quite a name—'

'Hang on, you two,' Mum says, and my heart sinks. I can read her tone these days before she's got to the point. This isn't going to be good. 'We haven't said you can join yet.' She looks at Dad.

His hands fall back by his sides. His smile drops too.

'What about schoolwork?' she says.

I grimace. 'What about it?' I mutter.

Bad move. Mum is scowling harder. 'Obi, this is serious.'

'The practices are mostly after school.' My voice comes out like a three-year-old's whine. 'I won't miss any classes.'

'Not until you're rich and touring the world!' says Dad, taking both of my hands and pushing them up near my face so that I'm air-trumpeting. 'Then you can start looking after me and your mother and your brothers. None of us will need to work again!'

Dad isn't helping. Mum rounds on him now. 'Can you be serious for one minute, please, Tumo?'

A silence drops so heavily that I'm sure even Bem and Jumoke can hear it from their bedroom. Bem's finally turned his music off.

Mum's an engineer; she's the lead designer of a massive shopping centre just south of London. It's a huge deal, but unless she gets these plans right, it will all come to nothing and millions of pounds of the company's money will have been wasted. She's been so stressed that she's turned into a bit of a monster. We have no idea what will set her off.

'Come on, darling,' Dad says. 'We should be encouraging her. What's wrong with Obi joining an after-school club?'

'After school is for homework,' Mum says.

'I'm only in Year 8,' I remind her. 'We don't get that much.'

'Remember when Jumoke wanted to get a paper round?' Mum barrels on. 'We discussed it and decided that if he woke up at 6 a.m. every Saturday he'd be tired for the rest of the week.'

'Mum . . .' I try again, but I know what she's like when she's in this mood. 'It's only until Christmas. It's not a big deal.'

It's a big deal to me.

'If it's not a big deal, don't do it,' Mum says.

Is it just me, or is she completely contradicting herself? 'How am I supposed to do something that *is* a big deal unless I start it in the first place?' I ask her. 'What if I'm destined to be a trumpeter?'

Mum raises a hand to cut me off. 'You have

to understand how important your education is.'

Once she starts on about the importance of education, there's no way I can win. I feel a lump rising in my throat. She just doesn't get how much I need this.

'Music is important too,' says Dad, his voice low.

He gets it.

Mum ignores him and keeps speaking to me. 'What you learn now sets you up for your GCSEs. Which set you up for your A levels. Which enable you to go to a good university and do a degree. Without a degree, well . . .' She gestures to Dad.

Dad looks like he's just been punched. Mum's face softens. 'Sorry, Tumo, I didn't mean—'

'What the hell *did* you mean?!' he yells.

'Just that you didn't go to university and now you don't have a job you love,' she says. She's trying to reverse-dig.

'What? A job that pays what yours does?' he shouts again.

'It's not—' she tries.

'I'm sorry that I didn't get a fancy degree,' he says. 'I'm sorry you earn more than me. I'm sorry I'm such a disappointment to you.'

'For God's sake!' Mum snaps back.

This is my fault, I know. I should never have brought up the music thing. While my mum was at university, Dad did low-paying jobs while he tried to make it as a jazz musician. But when he married Mum, and they had Jumoke, Dad had to take the job at the council to bring in a steady income. Because of marrying Mum, Dad gave up the thing in his life he loved most.

'Look, forget about it,' I snap. I want to join orchestra, but not if it's going to be just another thing for them to row about. It happens most nights these days. Sucker Punch is looking more appealing. They practise at lunch time so I could join them without ever having to ask permission.

'You're worried that Obi will turn out like me — only earning the low end of five figures.' He narrows his eyes and looks really mean. My eyes blur with tears. 'Newsflash, Shannon,' he says, 'some people aren't as concerned about money as you are. Some people would rather be happy than rich.'

'For once this isn't about you!' she says, her voice full of spite. 'I'm happy. I like my job.'

'I said, forget about it!' I say, wishing they'd stop.

'You *must* like your job,' he says. 'You like it more than your family!'

'I don't really want to be in orchestra anyway,' I say, softening my voice, trying a different tack. 'You're right, Mum. It will be too much hassle.'

'We have three actual children in this family,' she says to Dad. 'Why do you have to behave like the biggest child of them all?'

I've lost them. This started off being about me, but now it's about how much they hate each other. I back out of the room, turn and run up the stairs.

'Most of the time I feel like a single parent,' I hear Dad say as I reach the landing.

I slam my door and grab my trumpet again. I put my lips to the mouthpiece and start to play. Softly this time, so as not to get Mum even angrier. The rich sound of the song fills my ears and cuts out everything else. Surrounded by music I finally feel OK.

Dad's right: music is really important. And when he picked this family over a music career, I'm not at all sure he made the right choice.

Jumoke opens my door. 'Football?' he asks.

I shake my head.

'Come on,' he pleads.

I put my trumpet down. 'I don't know. There's some stuff I need to do on the computer.'

'Homework or social network?'

We both smile. Jumoke knows the deal with homework. He has even more than I do.

'Umm . . . both . . . neither . . .'

'Come on,' he says, opening the door wide to the bedroom he shares with Bem. 'Don't make me drag moanie boy out on my own.'

'Hey!' Bem protests, appearing at his shoulder.

Downstairs I hear that Mum hasn't finished with Dad quite yet. 'Couldn't you have at least loaded the dishwasher?'

'I'm coming,' I say.

Jumoke and Bem race down the stairs ahead of me, and I have to run to catch up.

'Mum! Dad! We're just off to play football,' Jumoke calls. 'Back before nine!' He's already opened the door as I get to the bottom.

'OK,' Dad says. 'See you then.'

Jumoke holds the door for me and I sprint out before Mum calls us back. I can just hear her saying, 'Have you even checked that they've done their homework? Or do I have to do that too?'

Hopefully, by the time we get back, Mum will have chilled out. I'm grateful to Jumoke for getting us out of there.

And then the truth hits me. This is what Jumoke does: he takes me and Bem to play football every time Mum and Dad argue. He's always done it. But he's had to do it loads more recently. When did my family start falling apart like this? And how the hell could I not have noticed?

Chapter 8

The next day I check all the usual places Donna hangs out at break. After the classroom and the music rooms, there's only one place she'll be. I push open the door to the girls' loos. Success.

Donna's staring at herself in the mirror, curling sections of her hair round her finger and making them into ringlets.

Sonia's standing behind her. 'The thing is,' Sonia's saying, 'dads are just so hard to buy for.'

They don't say hi or even look at me when I walk in, like I'm not worth bothering with.

'My dad's the worst,' Donna replies, not looking at Sonia, her eyes still fixed on her own reflection. 'I mean, he's been everywhere and has everything. What am I supposed to do? Buy moon rock?'

'That's a great idea!' says Sonia.

'I was joking,' says Donna, rolling her eyes and clearly getting sick of Sonia's bottom-licking.

I take a deep breath and cut in. 'Hi,' I say, hating that I actually feel nervous about speaking to a girl who's supposed to be my friend.

'What do you want?' barks Sonia. Sometimes she takes the lapdog thing too far.

'I want a word with Donna,' I say.

My parents have always told me I need to be honest and never lie. But some people don't deserve to know the truth. My parents are being idiots, so I'm going to join Sucker Punch and not tell them about it. Much simpler.

'Go ahead,' says Sonia.

Donna hasn't said anything, but she has stopped curling her hair.

'A *private* word,' I say. Then, remembering that this isn't Sonia's fault, I add, 'If you don't mind, please.'

Sonia looks at Donna, who waves her away with a flap of her hand. Amazingly Sonia obeys, heading out of the bathroom and saying, 'I'll see you in class, yeah?'

Donna nods.

I wait for Sonia to leave before starting. 'I wanted to speak to you about Sucker Punch,' I say. 'I'd really like to join . . . if you'll have me.'

'I thought you said you didn't want to be in my stupid band.'

I wince. 'I only said that because you guys ambushed me.'

Her face softens. She turns away from the mirror and looks me in the eye. 'I guess I deserved it,' she says, 'after being so rude.'

I'm unable to speak. Is this Donna, being . . . *nice*?

'Lenny asking us if you could join was just unexpected, that's all,' she says. 'We never talked about changing anything with the band. I didn't know Lenny thought we needed anyone else . . . I took it personally. Sorry.'

'I . . . er . . .' Now I'm really shocked. Donna *apologizing*? This is a first.

'And also it was a bit weird for me because we've always been a girl-fronted rock band. And the girl in a girl-fronted rock band always gets the most attention. With you in it we're just . . .

a band. I'm not the USP any more.'

'Come on, Donna,' I say. 'You'll still be the lead singer. You're still the prettiest person in Sucker Punch. By a mile. If Sucker Punch wants a USP, it is your amazing hair.'

Donna's hair is like brunette silk. It's thick and glossy and falls down her back in pretty waves. My hair is afro and black and never grows much past my shoulders. If I wanted smooth hair like hers, I would have to sew extensions into my hair and that's just too much time and hassle for someone like me.

Sometimes I wish I wasn't like someone like me.

Maybe it's time to change myself.

'Anyway,' she says, 'now that I've had time to think about it, I think you'd be a great addition. Both the sound of your trumpet, and you.'

It's not as flattering as being asked out by the fittest boy in the school, but being allowed to join the best band in the school is pretty up there.

'I'm in.' Should we high-five or something? 'I know Lenny mentioned I'm a big-band gal – but we don't have to go as far as Benny Goodman or anything.'

'Benny *who?*' she asks.

I cringe. Of course she hasn't heard of him. 'He's like the father of big band. The main name in the genre. But although I reckon Sucker Punch could incorporate some of his influences, we wouldn't need to change a lot.'

'Oh yeah,' she says. 'Lenny said about the big-band thing.'

I nod. 'Yeah, and—'

'Do you fancy Lenny?' She asks this like it's the most natural follow-up question in the world. Suddenly I wonder if she wants me in the band because she thinks I'm her enemy and wants to keep me close.

I wish things were simple like they used to be in my old school. I played football with the boys at break and most of the girls left me alone. No one accused me of fancying anyone because no one really fancied anyone. Hard to think that was in Year 7, only six months ago. I joined Hillcrest because it's the same school that my brothers went to. Here the boys surround the girls like smoke. It's choking. And it seems it's gone to a lot of the girls' heads. You can't sit next to a boy in class without someone asking if you fancy him. Because of my lack of best friend, I have to sit next to boys loads – but it doesn't mean I fancy them all!

'No. I don't fancy Lenny,' I tell her.

Donna smiles. 'Good,' she says. 'Cos that could get complicated.'

I don't know if she means because we would be in the same band or because it would create a love triangle.

Donna links her arm through mine and leads me out of the bathroom. 'So, if you're in the band, we're now band mates. Which means we're *mates* mates. Let's hang out.'

This is something I never thought would happen – me and Donna hanging out together. I'm not sure it's something I want, but I can't see a polite way out of this and I guess we do have to bond. She's probably keeping me close as an enemy, but I'd like to show her she has nothing to worry about. That I could be a friend.

'OK . . . that would be cool,' I say.

Chapter 9

Donna shows me into her kitchen. It's massive. Everything's bright white, the surfaces are clear and nothing's out on the counter. Not even cereal boxes or squash bottles or recipe books. It's the exact opposite to my house. Her Yorkshire terrier's in a little pen in the corner, jumping up and down and yapping for attention.

'Are your mum and dad in?' I ask her.

Donna shakes her head. 'Mum does yoga on Thursdays. And Dad's . . . not here.'

'Where is he?' I ask.

I think I see Donna stifle a wince, but she spins round and picks up the dog from its pen.

I lean over and stroke it. It's got a pink bow holding back its fringe.

'What's her name?' I ask.

'*His* name,' Donna says. 'Harry.'

The poor dog scratches at his pink bow.

'So Obi Wan,' Donna says, putting the dog back, 'what do you want to drink?'

'I don't know,' I say, ignoring the Star Wars reference — it's not as if I haven't heard it a million times before. Harry sits in his bed and eyes me. 'What have you got?'

'Hot chocolate . . . Coffee . . . What do you drink when you're hanging out with Lenny?'

So she's still stuck on that. I'm guessing that's why I'm here. 'We hardly hang out,' I tell her. 'We did. Just that once.'

'Just that once?' Donna asks, her face trying not to crumble.

'You really haven't got anything to worry about when it comes to me and Lenny — promise.'

Donna beams, showing all her teeth. This is not her practised smile, and it looks much prettier.

'I don't mind what we drink,' I tell her.

'Two hot chocolates coming up!' she says. She starts opening cupboards and taking out loads of different tins and jars. 'I make the best hot chocolate in town. Prepare to be blown away.'

'I'll wear a seat belt.' And I mime clicking one on.

'So, are you excited about your first band practice?' she asks me, pouring chocolate sprinkles into a massive mug. 'We're meeting up on Sunday in Joel's garage. Have you seen Joel's garage? It's awesome. It has plug sockets and everything for amps. And there are even beanbags and an old sofa for us to chill out on when we have a break.'

'I imagine if it's Joel's *old* sofa, then it must be pretty gross.'

Donna laughs. 'He puts the *gunge* into grunge, doesn't he?'

I laugh too. I like Joel, but I don't think I've ever seen him wearing anything that isn't stained or creased – usually both. She presses a button on a fancy machine that looks like a slightly smaller version of the ones they have in Starbucks.

'Wait till you see it yourself,' she says. 'And if his mum's around on Sunday—'

'There's a little problem,' I blurt out.

'A little problem with what?'

'With practising,' I say.

Donna stops, a spoon of Nutella hovering over the mug.

I gulp. I don't know how Donna will react when I tell her I can't join in on any out-of-school rehearsals. Will she kick me out when I've only just been allowed in?

'I'm not going to be able to do much after school or at weekends,' I tell her.

'Why not?' she asks.

'My mum won't let me.'

Donna creases her forehead. She dips the spoon of Nutella into the cup and starts stirring. 'But it's only a few hours.'

I sigh. '*I* know that! But my mum is a schoolwork Nazi! She'll think I'm going to fail at everything I do for the rest of my life if I turn up to a few band rehearsals in my free time. She doesn't think I should *have* any free time!'

'What would she prefer you do?' Donna asks, going to the fridge for a can of squirty cream. 'Sit on the sofa all day?'

'I don't know . . .' My words trail off as I think back to last night's argument. At breakfast this morning, everything was normal – as in, no one said a word about the fact my parents had been screaming the house down so badly we had to run out. This is how we deal with our issues at home: we don't.

I've heard girls talk to each other about feelings and emotions and stuff. And there is no one I know who has more feelings and emotions than Donna. If I'm going to change myself, maybe this is a good place to start.

'Are you all right, Obi?' she asks.

The high-pitchedness in her voice has gone. I'm not sure, but my instinct says she sincerely wants to know if I'm OK.

'Umm . . .' I take a deep breath and it's shaky when I exhale. 'Not really,' I say. 'It's just . . .'

'Come on,' she says, her voice almost a whisper now. 'You can tell me.'

Can I? I do want to tell someone. But I'm not sure how close we are yet. 'My parents had a fight last night. It was pretty colossal.'

'Really? Why?'

I'm going to have to edit this story so there's

no mention of orchestra. What's one more little secret?

'My mum doesn't want me to do music. She doesn't think it's important. But music is my dad's whole life – or at least it would be if he hadn't made the mistake of marrying Mum and having us.'

'Poor you,' she says, sounding really sympathetic. 'Are they going to split up?'

'No!' I yelp. That thought hadn't even crossed my mind. But now I think about it, why wouldn't they? 'At least . . . I don't think so.'

'One in three marriages ends in divorce,' Donna adds.

My head starts to spin. How did I not think of this as a possibility? I really don't want my parents to break up. But they fight so often.

'That means that two in three are fine,' I say, to reassure myself more than anything.

'Let's do the maths,' says Donna, 'with the people we know.'

This seems a bit sick, but I'm suddenly desperate for some kind of science to hang this on. 'Maxie and Tara's mum and dad are divorced. Sonia's parents?' I ask Donna.

'Together,' she says.

'Candy's?' I ask.

Candy lives next door to Donna so she knows the family pretty well.

'Together,' she says.

'Hannah?'

'Together.'

'I don't think Indiana's parents are married,' I say. 'But they live in the same house. How does that fit with our figures?'

'Don't know,' she says. 'I think we have to count that as together.'

'So out of our seven friends and their six sets of parents,' I say, holding up six fingers, 'only one pair are divorced.' I drop a finger. 'So the odds are: my parents will be next.'

'The stats never lie,' Donna says flatly.

I laugh, but it's not funny. It was pretty nasty that I hoped my friends' parents would be divorced so that mine would stay together.

'Please tell me your parents argue as much as mine do.'

Donna twirls and beams, this time doing her supermodel smile. 'Sorry, Obi,' she says, batting her eyelashes. 'We're one happy family.' She points to a vase of flowers on the counter. 'My dad gets them for my mum all the time.'

The odds of my parents divorcing are rising by the second.

'This is depressing,' I say.

'Come on.' Donna squeezes my arm tightly and forces some joy into her voice. 'I think we have ice cream in the freezer.'

'It's the middle of December!' I say.

'If it was summer, I'd have eaten it already!'

I laugh. Donna pushes the mug of hot chocolate towards me as well as a jar full of mini-marshmallows. I start pouring them in.

Even though the problem hasn't been solved I feel a little lighter from telling her about it. Should I tell her more about the weird stuff going on in my head?

'Do you know what, Donna?' I start. 'Sometimes I think my parents' fights are all my fault.' My parents have always argued, but the arguments have got a lot worse as I've got older.

'What if my dad resents us kids? Do you think I'm weird for thinking that?'

Donna bites her lip like she's about to say something.

'Do you ever think you're weird?' I ask her. 'Do you ever think that if you acted differently, things would be better?' There's a lump in my throat like I'm about to cry.

Donna leans forward and strokes my arm. 'Do you know what, Obi?' she says, looking into my eyes.

'What?'

'You don't need to tell everyone everything that's going on in your life,' she says.

'Huh?' Donna's always telling everyone everything about *her* life. Why is she telling me not to?

'It's true!' she says. 'If you're worried about people thinking you're weird, don't say it. If something stressful is going on and you tell people, they'll only bring it up and ask you questions about it and upset you when you're not prepared. Much better to keep it to yourself.'

This advice is hard to believe coming from

the girl who has never kept anything to herself! But then, maybe she's right. How am I ever going to get a best friend if people find out how insane I can be? I don't have to open up my crazy little head. My parents say I should be honest, but maybe they're wrong. Dishonesty is so much simpler.

'Oh my God!' she suddenly shouts, snapping me out of my thoughts. 'We should totally straighten your hair.'

And now we don't have to talk about the stressful, annoying stuff that's going on in my life. By hanging out with Donna, I'm not stuck dealing with my own thoughts all the time – I'm just having fun.

If this is what having a close friend is like, it feels pretty good.

Chapter 10

The next morning I head for the equipment huts where I know I'll find the girls. Most mornings in winter we huddle in this corner where the two huts meet, sheltering from the cold. Donna picked this as our hanging-out spot because from here we can see the football pitch. And, more importantly, the boys on the football pitch.

I take a deep breath before I round the corner. I'm not sure what they're going to say, but I know this is about to be a big deal.

'Hi, Obi,' says Hannah, then she literally does a double take.

The others turn round and their mouths drop open, eyes wide. If I wasn't so worried about being the centre of attention, it would be comical.

'Hiiiiiiii, Oooooooooobiiiiiiiiiii,' says Candy, drawing out her greeting so it's really long and comes out like a question. She smiles. 'Is there something different about you today?'

'Obi, your hair looks amazing!' Tara doesn't mess around.

'You look gorgeous,' says Abby, pulling self-consciously at her new short haircut. 'Really, really nice.'

Indiana, with her long plaited hair, says, 'You should straighten your hair all the time.'

'When did you do that?' asks Maxie.

I glance at Donna and she's beaming her toothy grin. I used to think this look was smugness, but now I see it's pride in her work. As well as an excellent singer and perfect looks, beauty regimes are another of her talents.

'Last night,' I tell them.

Last night with Donna was actually really fun. But when I think back on it, we didn't really *do* anything. We got ice cream, then went to eat it in her room. Her room is amazing; she's got a double bed, a massive TV, a million Blu-rays and speakers that can control her music from anywhere in the house apparently. She has a really cool collection of china dolls, which she's not ashamed of because they go back almost all her life and some of them are antiques. Her dad travels a lot and he always brings her back a present from wherever he goes, and it's always something expensive.

My room is nothing like hers. I have the smallest room in the house because Bem and Jumoke have to share. It only just fits a small wardrobe and my single bed. Even Harry the dog's bed is posher than mine. It's a four-poster!

After drooling over all her stuff, Donna sat me down in front of her dressing-table mirror — lined with light bulbs like something out of a movie star's dressing room — and brought out her equipment.

'Have you ever straightened your hair before?' she asked.

Candy's sister did it for me for Tara and Maxie's party a few months ago, but I've never done it myself. I have no idea how to. Thing is, I guess it's a kind of mother–daughter thing you learn, but my mum's hair isn't like mine. Mine is afro, while hers is smooth and blonde. She's learned how to plait mine up into cornrows, but that's about it. It's not that I prefer her hair – I just wish we had the *same* hair so she could help me.

'Do you know how to do it on afro hair?' I asked Donna.

'Pur-lease!' she said with a laugh. She lifted up the straighteners and comb. 'There's nothing I can't do with these babies!' Then she leaned closer and whispered in my ear, 'And I might have YouTubed it.'

I laughed. It was so nice that she'd prepared for me coming over. She brought all this stuff out of her drawers – hair oil, straightening balm, heat-protect spray. All this stuff I hadn't even heard of.

Then we worked together, undoing my cornrows.

'Warning siren,' I said, 'my hair's really, really big when it's loose.'

Donna shook her head quickly. 'Nothing shocks me, *dahleeng*,' she said in a French accent, like she was a fancy chef. 'If I don't get to be famous myself, I want to be a make-up artist to the stars. I have to get into training to make sure I'm unshockable!' She gave a flourish of her hand.

Who knew that Donna could be silly?

True to her word, she didn't laugh or say anything about my massive hair when it was unleashed. Then she separated it out into sections and straightened each bit. It took over an hour. We talked the whole time – not about my family issues, not even about Lenny – but about, well, *nothing* really. Donna is quite funny when she wants to be. She said she's an only child which means she's spoiled rotten and she's not ashamed of it. She was never lonely growing up. If her parents weren't around then she just went into her room and kept herself amused with all her stuff. And she was allowed to have people over any time . . .

'That's why Mum always keeps ice cream in the freezer, so I can entice friends round. Just like tonight.'

So Donna thinks of me as a friend. And this side of Donna made me want to be her friend too.

When my hair was done she held up a second

mirror behind me so I could see the full force of her handiwork.

'You look errr-maze-ing!!!' she said, clapping her hands.

It was amazing; I looked really different. I looked good.

Right now, the girls approach me like a gang of zombies – all reaching for my hair.

'Can I touch it?' asks Indiana.

I laugh. 'Of course. It's not going to break!' Then I look at Donna. 'It won't, will it?' I ask her, half under my breath.

Donna giggles and shakes her head. 'No,' she says. 'Silly.'

The zombies pause. Sonia turns and looks at Donna. 'Did you do this?' she asks.

Donna nods. 'Yup. Cool, huh?'

Sonia's eyebrows bunch in the middle. 'When? Last night?'

Donna nods again.

Candy gasps. 'You were round at Donna's last night?' she asks. 'How come you didn't invite me?'

'Umm . . .' I start. I had no idea there was

so much politics in girls' friendships. When do you invite one friend over and not others? There are nine of us girls. Does that mean we have to do everything as a group of nine all the time?

Donna links arms with me. 'It was just us two hanging out last night,' she says. 'Is that OK with you, Candy?'

Candy looks a little embarrassed, but I don't blame her for asking. Of course we're all part of the Boys' School Girls, but me and Donna have never been close. And no one would put us together because they don't know we have anything in common. The only pair that hangs out without the others is Tara and Abby, as far as I know. And that's because they've been best friends since forever.

Tara examines me closely, like she's wondering if I've had a stroke. 'Are you friends with Donna now?' she asks.

I look at Donna and we share a smile because I know that I am. 'Yup,' I say.

Tara and Abby went to the same primary school as Donna and they know what she used to be like. I think they know too much. There's a nicer side to Donna and it's one I'm just starting to see.

'We're best friends,' says Donna, pulling me into her so I almost stumble.

I laugh at her being so forceful. But none of the other girls are laughing.

Then I realize what she just said.

Donna just called me her *best friend*.

I choke. I don't mean to but . . . I was just starting to get my head round being friends with Donna. Now she's calling me her *best* friend.

'That's right, isn't it, Obi Wan?' she says to me.

I'm too shocked to reply. We both like music, but not the same kind. Donna's quite superficial, only concerned with her hair and her looks and Lenny. And I get the feeling she only likes him because he's the best-looking boy in our year.

But then again, I suppose best friends spend hours straightening hair and never complain about their arms hurting. Best friends give each other ice cream and never make them talk about their feelings and problems if they don't want to.

If she's changing me, maybe I could change her. I'll have to work on making her less boy crazy and less mean to people.

My instinct kicks in, saying it doesn't quite *feel* like we're best friends, but then again I've never had a best friend before, so how would my instinct know? If she says she is, and I act like she is, the feeling could come later.

'Damn right!' I say. 'Total besties.'

This is what I've always wanted. A best friend that's there for me first, before anyone else. I feel a sunny glow inside me even though it's only five degrees today. I look at Donna and she raises her eyebrows − a secret best-friend look that I've seen Tara and Abby do.

It makes me so happy. If I can make this work, I'll get the best friend I've always wanted. Who would have thought it would be Donna?

But then I catch Sonia's face and my happiness fades. Sonia looks as if she's just watched her cat get hit by a car. I guess she always assumed *she* was Donna's best friend. Now Donna has wiped her off like pen on a whiteboard.

I didn't think about Sonia. And neither did

Donna. That's what makes it worse — she didn't even cross our minds.

'Sonia . . .' I start.

'I've got to go,' she says. 'Homework.'

She runs inside and I know what me and Donna have just done — we've broken her heart.

'Should we go after her?' I say to Donna.

'Why?' says Donna.

She can't be that oblivious. 'I think she's upset,' I say, as if she didn't know.

'She'll get over it.' Donna pulls me towards the school doors. 'Sit with me in geography, yeah?'

As she drags me inside I try to convince her to speak to Sonia and see if she's all right, but Darnell Wade from Year 10 looks at her and she flips her hair at him. I don't think she's listening to me so I give up for now.

I've always wanted a best friend. But I'm not sure I want it like this.

Chapter 11

Donna leans over my desk and looks at my page. 'That's not right,' she says.

I look down at my sums and try to see what she means. I'm not surprised they aren't right – I can't do maths to save my life – but what surprises me is that Donna can see the mistakes so quickly.

'How do you know?' I whisper to her.

'Don't tell anyone,' she says, 'but I've got simultaneous equations totally nailed. I'm like Einstein. Just with better hair.'

I burst out laughing.

'Er . . . girls!' Mrs Grabovski says to us. 'No talking, please.'

Donna and I put our heads down instantly, but we're still giggling.

Sonia, who had to sit next to David Cotton because I took her place next to Donna, stares back at us. I feel bad, but what can I do? I want to trust Donna, but the way she dumped Sonia for me so easily fills me with worry. And this sudden wish to be my best friend only started after I started hanging out with Lenny. My instinct is telling me to be careful.

I tell my instinct to shut up.

'Here. Copy mine,' Donna whispers, and she turns her book a little so it's easier to see what she's written.

It's been about five hours since Donna told everyone I'm her best friend, and since then we've been inseparable. We've sat next to each other in every lesson – all except RE, which we have in different classes, and biology, where Mr Warne makes us sit in alphabetical order. I feel like an old-fashioned princess whose dance card is all booked up. There's no more panic about who I'm going to have to sit next to. No more hanging round boys that pick their nose. And, most unexpectedly of all, I'm really starting to like Donna.

And if she lets me copy her maths – even better!

It might not feel properly right yet, but it'll come, I'm sure of it.

I'm in the middle of scribbling down the work from her page when there's a knock on the classroom door and in walks Miss Rotimi. The whole class draws in a huge breath because she is so beautiful – or maybe it's just me. She's wearing a yellow dress with white flowers on it and a white woollen cardigan.

'Sorry to interrupt, Mrs Grabovski,' she says.

'I think Miss Rotimi must be one of the most stylish people in the world,' I whisper.

Donna nods. 'Yeah, you're right. Not many people could pull of that bright shade of yellow – especially in winter – but she's got it spot on.'

I *hmm* in agreement.

Mrs Grabovski is asking Miss Rotimi how the Christmas concert is coming along, so we can sort of get away with whispering to each other.

'Except you,' says Donna. 'You could probably work that colour.'

I beam at the comparison to Miss Rotimi. There is no way I could ever be as beautiful as her, but if I could just borrow her fashion sense, that would be awesome.

'I'm going to buy a hairband like that,' I tell Donna.

'You totally should!' Donna says. 'I'll help you style it if you like.'

'Thanks.' This is absolutely best-friend behaviour.

'Actually,' Miss Rotimi says, 'about the Christmas concert . . . I was wondering if I could have a quick word with one of the students.'

We all look around, wondering who she's going to pick. Some of the boys blush when Miss Rotimi's eyes land on them. Boys are such weaklings when it comes to beautiful women.

Then Miss Rotimi looks at me. 'There you are,' she says.

I put my hand to my chest. *'Me?'* I realize I'm blushing.

Miss Rotimi nods and holds out her arm gracefully. 'Could we have a little chat outside, please? It won't take a moment.'

I look at Mrs Grabovski, who nods. 'Go on then — these sums can wait till you get back.'

I look down at Donna, who whispers, 'Lucky,' under her breath. Getting out of maths – even just for five minutes – is better than cake. I stick out my tongue at Donna, pretending to boast, then follow Miss Rotimi from the room.

Alone in the corridor with her, I feel shy. I can see all the boys in the classroom trying to look at us through the window, and I shuffle round a little so my back's to the door.

'Obi,' Miss Rotimi says, 'how are you?'

'I'm fine, thank you,' I say slowly. This is not how I expected this conversation to start. Teachers hardly ever ask how you are. 'How are you?' This feels like a friendly chat.

She smiles at me. 'Fine . . . Looking forward to the weekend!' But then the smile drops and she bites her lip. 'Actually I'm not fine at all.'

'What's the matter?' I ask.

'The Christmas concert is just over two weeks away and I'm desperately short of brass.' Her frown turns into a smile and I see I've fallen for her trick. 'There was one student – a very talented one – who said she'd sign up, but then I never saw her again.'

I look at the floor.

Miss Rotimi pushes me gently by the shoulder. 'Come on, Obi,' she says. 'Please join orchestra.'

It was really fun for the one night. But Mum won't let me. Then Mum and Dad had that huge argument. And orchestra's not cool; the people in it get teased . . . so much so that Lenny won't join either.

'I don't know,' I reply.

'Oh, please, Obi,' she says. 'Us girls need to stick together. Besides, I know your dad would be proud to see you up there onstage.'

My head snaps up in surprise. How does she know about my dad being into music?

'A famous trumpeter like him would be happy to see his daughter following in his footsteps.'

'I don't know about *famous*,' I say, rolling my eyes.

'Oof, don't let him hear you say that!' she says, chuckling. 'Men and their egos, you know.'

I *do* know. I saw the effects of Dad's bruised ego the other day. But what's weird is that Miss Rotimi knows all this stuff about my family.

Lenny used to do music lessons with her so he knows her. Did *he* go and tell her about me and about my dad being a famous trumpeter? I didn't realize he was paying such close attention.

He must have been the 'little bird' who told her I played the trumpet.

'You're smiling!' Miss Rotimi says.

Am I?

'That means you want to join. That means you *have to* join.'

'I don't know . . .' I say. '. . . my parents.'

Miss Rotimi flaps her hands. 'Come to practice tomorrow night at least. I have something I want to give you.'

What could Miss Rotimi want to give me? For a moment I wonder if she could have heard me and Donna talking about her hairband and she plans to give me hers. I don't want to be a teacher's pet, but I do want to help her out.

'OK,' I say. 'I'll come.' I'll have to tell Mum I'm doing a homework thing.

She clasps her hands together.

'Just tomorrow,' I say, coming to my senses.

'We'll see . . .' There is a twinkle in her eye

and I know she thinks she can persuade me to do anything.

It's easy to keep Sucker Punch from my parents, but orchestra will be hard to hide because of all the after-school practices. And I'll have to lie to the girls too. Still, it's only for a few weeks. Maybe I can invent a school project to cover my tracks with my parents and a family thing to cover my tracks with my friends.

Miss Rotimi looks up at the ceiling, as if thanking God. 'Obi, you are my new favourite. Thank you.' She hurries away down the corridor. Then she turns back and holds her finger out to me. 'I'll see you tomorrow,' she says. 'After school. Don't forget.' And she's off again.

How could I forget? Miss Rotimi has made me feel really special. And she's going to give me something too. I wonder what? I hope it isn't extra homework.

My mind flashes with an image of telling Lenny all about it and laughing with him. I push that thought away – If I'm going to try to make this best-friends-with-Donna thing work, then I have to not think about him any more. It's the

Girl Code. I think about Donna instead. Will she disown me as her best friend as soon as she finds out I've done something as lame as sign up to orchestra?

I guess this is just another little secret I've got to keep. Like Donna says, I don't have to tell everyone everything.

Chapter 12

The orchestra sounds amazing. I blast out my trumpet as we play *Deck the Halls*, and it almost feels like we're in an old country church with snow all around us. When we all get the notes right like this I sort of forget who I am for a moment, and all there is is the music, filling me up from the inside. It's the best feeling in the world.

Miss Rotimi is conducting, floating around the room as she points to each section – brass, wind, strings – letting us know when it's our turn to come in. With the way her arms are wafting around, her stick like a wand, she looks like a fairy godmother granting wishes.

As it's a Christmas concert, I pretty much know all the pieces we're doing – they are just the regular standard carols and stuff. All I have to do is catch up on the arrangements Miss

Rotimi's organized. It's hard work, but hearing how great we sound makes it easier. I practised a few in my bedroom last night.

We finish off the song and Miss Rotimi gives us a smile so wide it makes me smile. I look around; everyone else is smiling too.

I catch Lenny's eye. He's over the other side of the hall, by the string section. He winks at me.

I did a double take when he came in at the beginning of practice. I still can't believe he's here, after he said he wouldn't join. Part of me wonders if he told Miss Rotimi to get me to come because he's decided to come too . . . but then I tell myself not to be stupid.

'Well, Hillcrest High,' Miss Rotimi says to us, 'that was really very good. We need to work on our entrances and cut-offs to make them cleaner and crisper. You have to make sure you watch me carefully so you know exactly when to come in. But you're doing marvellously. I know we only have a couple of weeks until the concert itself . . .'

A muttering starts up among the group. The

boy next to me says, 'A couple of weeks! That's so soon.'

'What about me?' I say back. 'I just got here!'

'But I also know . . .' says Miss Rotimi, raising her voice just a little, 'that we'll all be completely and one hundred per cent ready by then.'

A groan from us says we're not so sure. I want it all to sound good for the concert. I want everyone listening to feel how I feel when I play — to drift away to another place as the music wraps itself round them. But if we're not note-perfect it'll just be a shambles.

'Go on,' she says, 'we're done. Have a great weekend, people.'

Everyone starts packing up. I reach down and get my case from just beside me. Playing today felt wonderful; it gave me everything I was missing. So as long as no one finds out . . .

I told Mum and Dad I'm doing a homework project with Donna tonight, and I told Donna my parents wanted me home for a family thing. I'm lying all over the place. I know there's a chance Mum and Dad will find out about the orchestra – and they'll know for definite if they decide to come along to the Christmas concert – but I'll cross that bridge when I come to it.

I take the mouthpiece off my trumpet and slot it into its place in the case.

'Is that complicated?'

Lenny's hovering over me.

'We cover it in the first lesson,' I say to him, grinning. 'They make you piece together a Boeing 747, and if the jet flies, you're allowed to move on to trumpets.'

I love the way he always laughs at my bad jokes.

'Nah, not really.' I put the trumpet in and close the lid. 'That's all I have to do.'

'This is even easier.' He takes the chain off his neck, threads on the purple pick and fastens it round his neck again.

'What's that?' I ask him.

'A guitar pick,' he says.

'Well, duh,' I reply, rolling my eyes.

'It's my *lucky* guitar pick,' he says. 'The only

time I'm not wearing it round my neck is when I'm using it to play.'

I turn my back on him to get my coat from the back of my chair. It's difficult to know what to say to Lenny, especially as Donna has made me promise to report back on everything he says. It's like she's got CCTV on us.

'My mum's coming to pick me up tonight. Want a lift?' he asks.

'Umm . . .' I think about it for a second. I suppose there's no harm. I can grill him for information on Donna's behalf. See if I can find out how he feels about her. 'Yeah,' I say. Then I realize that sounded rude. 'Yes, please.'

Lenny smiles. He waits for me to get the rest of my stuff and we head for the door.

'What are you doing this weekend?' he asks.

'Oh, you know, the usual,' I say.

'And that is?'

'Trying to stop Bem and Jumoke from killing each other,' I say. 'Then, when I can't take any more, try to kill them myself.' My life sounds pretty tragic when I say it out loud – and I haven't even mentioned my warring parents.

'How come you came?' I ask him. 'I thought you said you couldn't handle the mick being taken out of you.'

Lenny rubs his cheek. 'I thought of you.'

I turn my face so he can't see me blushing.

'You said you should go after the things you want,' he says. 'And if you can be brave and risk discovery, I can too.'

So that's all he meant. I'm sort of relieved.

'Don't worry,' I say, tapping my nose. 'It's our secret.'

Lenny looks relieved. 'Thank you.' He looks at his watch. 'Come on – Mum will be waiting.'

'Obi!'

I spin round to face Miss Rotimi. She's looking at me as she packs up her papers, getting them into her cute little tote bag.

'Miss?' I ask.

'Can you come here for a second, please?'

Oh yeah! I was so distracted by Lenny that I forgot that she wanted to give me something after practice today. I turn back to Lenny to ask him to wait, but I can see he's looking at his watch again.

'Don't worry,' I say. 'You go and meet your mum. See you Monday.'

He runs off out of the room and it's just me and Miss Rotimi in the hall. It feels massive.

'Hi, Miss Rotimi,' I say to her, feeling shy. She said I was her favourite, and for some reason this makes me feel self-conscious. Part of that centre-of-attention thing, I guess.

'How did you find it tonight?' she asks me. She's finished with the papers and she's got one hand resting in her bag and one on her hip.

'It was good!' I say, beaming. 'I've got some catching up to do, but it went OK. I think.'

'You did great,' she says, and I feel really proud of myself. I've never been singled out by a teacher like this before. I'm pretty average at everything in school, and I've always thought I was pretty average at the trumpet too.

'I told your dad you'd be excellent,' she says, looking to the ceiling.

'Huh?' I stop and look at her. Then I want to hide my surprise, so I carry on, but slowly. 'You've met my dad?'

'Yes!' she says, laughing at me as if I must be stupid. 'Didn't I say? We go to the same jazz club.'

I feel stupid. All this time I thought she thought I was special. Now I know she's only singled me out because she's friends with Dad.

'He talks about you and your brothers all the time,' she says.

I feel even more stupid because I've just realized my dad is the 'little bird' she mentioned. That's how she knew I played the trumpet and wanted me to join orchestra. It makes a lot more sense than Lenny taking the time to ask a teacher to include me.

'So you like jazz, Miss Rotimi?' I ask her, wondering how well she knows my dad.

'You don't think I listen to Christmas carols all year round, do you?'

I laugh. 'I guess not. It's just, you seem . . . cooler . . . than the regular jazz fan.'

'Ha!' she says. 'Slightly offended on behalf of jazz fans, but also touched that you think I'm cool.'

Now I'm even more embarrassed because I've just told a teacher I think she's cool.

'Jazz is my passion,' she says. 'I play the saxophone and always wanted to be a famous jazz musician.'

'My mum says there is no such thing as a *famous* jazz musician,' I joke.

Miss Rotimi doesn't smile. 'I bet your dad loves it when she says stuff like that.' She rolls her eyes in the same way Dad does.

'I've had jazz thrown at me from the day I was born, but Mum says if you asked the average person to name a jazz player, they wouldn't be able to.'

'But that just makes us better than average, doesn't it?' She winks at me like we're in on the same joke. I smile but realize that we're sort of insulting my mum.

'Which reminds me,' Miss Rotimi says, 'I wanted to give you something, didn't I?' She taps her bag, then bends over to rifle through it. She brings out an old vinyl record in a cardboard sleeve.

'Do you know what this is?'

'Of course,' I say. 'My dad has a ton of them.'

'Most people have MP3 players these days,' she says to me. 'And I have one of those too. But real music lovers collect these things. They're the best way to listen to music — if you can't catch it live, that is.'

She's gone off into that trance-like state that my dad goes into when he talks about jazz. It's a bit cringe really, but it's also quite sweet.

I'm so pleased she thinks of me as a 'real music lover'. She wants me to have this vinyl record. It'll be the start of my collection. Maybe one day I'll have thousands and they'll be worth loads because they're so old.

'What is it?' I ask her.

'It's a rare piece of jazz by a man called Bobby Benson. He's Nigerian. I think you'd really like him.'

She hands the record to me and I take it carefully in both hands. On the front there's a picture of a man playing the piano. Maybe this'll be the piece of music that makes me get jazz the same way Dad gets it. The same way I get big band.

'Thanks, Miss Rotimi,' I say. 'I'll be really careful with it.'

I study the cover like it's covered in winning lottery numbers.

'And make sure you memorize the smile on your dad's face when you give it to him,' she says. 'I'll want a full description.'

My heart sinks – again. This is for my dad. Why would I think I was special enough for her to give *me* a gift? I'm such an idiot.

'I've got to go.' I'm not sticking round for a second longer – my ego's too bruised.

'Let me know exactly what he says,' she tells me.

I hold the record in front of me like a muddy football as I head out of the hall and down the few little stairs to the main corridor. I stuck around for that! I gave up a lift home with Lenny's mum for *that*! I should call my dad and get him to pick me up – this is his fault really. Then I remember that I told my parents I was studying at Donna's house.

I grab my phone, about to call Donna and tell her what happened. Then I remember that

I'm not telling Donna about orchestra. She might laugh at me and change her mind about being my best friend like she changed her mind about Sonia.

Keeping all these secrets isn't as simple as I thought. Neither is having a best friend.

As I jump down from the last stair something falls out of the sleeve of the record. Oh great! I told Miss Rotimi I'd be careful and I've already failed. Standard behaviour from me.

It's a piece of paper. I put my trumpet case down so I can pick it up. When I do, I see it's a torn out bit of sheet music, but there are no notes on it – just handwritten words.

It was great seeing you the other
night. Can we do it again sometime?
Sometime SOON?

Love I x

Who's *I*?

It must be Miss Rotimi. But why is she sending my dad this message? In secret? They've met up before – maybe she just means bumping

117

into each other at the jazz club. But she's put a kiss. They're both Nigerian – they have that in common – so there's probably a simple explanation to all this, I tell myself.

But that doesn't stop me wondering:

Is my dad having an affair with Miss Rotimi?

I screw the note up into a ball. On my way out of the building, I throw the note in the bin.

Chapter 13

We're all sitting in front of the TV – it's the usual Saturday-night rubbish. Bem is on the floor, desperate for the adverts to come on because me and him are competing to see who can guess the name of the product first. Jumoke is taking up a whole armchair because he's about two foot taller than the rest of us. And I'm wedged between Mum and Dad.

'It's nice to spend some family time together, isn't it?' says Mum.

I'm about to say that watching Ant and Dec hardly counts as *family time*, but when I look up Mum's on her laptop, staring at the screen. There's a buzzing from Dad's pocket. So much for family time.

Dad stands, using me to push himself up.

'Hey!' I say.

But he doesn't notice as he checks his phone,

then takes the call on his way out of the room. I look over suspiciously. Who calls at nine o'clock on a Saturday night? Why couldn't he take the call in front of us?

It's Miss Rotimi. I know it is.

'Mum,' I begin.

What do I say to her? *Careful, I think Dad's having an affair with my music teacher.* But my family don't do the direct and honest approach.

'Hmm,' she replies. I say *replies*, but she doesn't look up from her computer.

If direct and honest isn't happening, I'll have to put another plan into action.

'Do you like jazz?' I ask her.

'It's OK,' she says, still looking at the screen.

'I hate it,' Bem says. 'It's just a load of notes slammed together.'

It's very sweet of Bem to chime in, but I have an agenda here!

'Have you ever tried to sit through a whole jazz song?' he says. 'You're waiting for it to end but you have no idea when it's going to end because there's no pattern to it – no chorus, no verses, no bridge. Then when it finally does, it comes as a surprise. *Hallelujah! I've been saved!'*

Jumoke starts laughing.

Mum, with the conversational heat off her, has forgotten we're here again.

'What about the dance crap that you listen too?' Jumoke says to Bem. 'It's exactly the same thing – just a load of beats, over and over, with no variation.'

'What about you, Mum?' I ask again, trying to get my plan back on track. 'Do you ever listen to Dad's jazz with him?'

'Erm, not much,' she says.

'When was the last time you gave it a go?' I say, sounding a little desperate now. 'Maybe it's like me and broccoli. Didn't like it all my life, tried it again last year and now I love it.'

'Hmm,' Mum says, eyes on her screen.

'So, Mum – ' I'm pleading for her attention – 'What do you think?'

'Mum thinks that she wants to buy me some decks,' says Bem.

'Get real,' says Jumoke. 'Do you know how much those things cost?'

'It'll be worth it when I'm a top DJ,' Bem says. He looks at Mum but she's still absorbed in her work. 'Won't it, Mum?'

All of us have turned to her. She's completely oblivious.

'Mum,' I nudge her.

Nothing.

'Mum!' I yell.

She jolts. Then frowns at me. 'What?'

I glare back at her, then at her laptop, trying to let her know how rude she's being. But perhaps grumpiness isn't the best way to get her onside.

'Mum,' I say again, this time more softly, 'do you ever go to Dad's jazz clubs with him?'

'They aren't really my thing.' Face back down at laptop.

'But maybe they *could* be your thing,' I push. 'Maybe if you gave them a chance, you'd like them.'

'I don't think so, Obi,' she says. 'The clubs are full of men having too much to drink and dancing badly and the music's always too loud.'

I imagine Miss Rotimi in there with her young, beautiful friends, dancing with all the drunk men.

'Don't diss Dad's dancing,' says Jumoke. 'He thinks he's the black Fred Astaire.'

They chuckle. When we call Dad on his bad dancing he says it's his slippers, or the floor, but we all know it's him.

'But, Mum,' I say, and I can hear the whiney tone in my voice, 'maybe you would get to like the clubs if you went more often. Maybe if you gave it some real *effort*—'

Mum huffs at me. 'What are you harping on about, Obi? I can't be off clubbing every night with your father – who would look after you three?'

'I'll do it!' says Jumoke. 'I won't even charge much.'

Bem tuts. 'The house would've spontaneously combusted by the time they got to the station.'

'It's not like he goes *every* night,' I say, ignoring my stupid brothers. 'Or even every weekend. And we're old enough to look after ourselves once in a while,' I say. 'You and Dad should hang out together more often. Have some fun.'

Mum sighs. 'Look, Obi, I have a lot on at the moment. Until this shopping-centre project is sorted, I can't think of anything else. Certainly not clubbing.'

'But—'

'Please just let me get back to this,' she says.

Conversation over. Mum's useless. I get up and storm out of the room. I bet she hasn't even noticed.

I hear Dad talking quietly in the kitchen. I creep down the hallway and try to listen in.

'I don't know if I can . . .' he's saying.

Is he talking to Miss Rotimi right now? I assumed she didn't have his number, or else why would she be passing notes to him through me. But maybe she got it somehow. Maybe she's telling him about the record she gave me to give to him. For a second I worry that he'll shout at me for not handing it over. But then he would have to explain why a pretty young teacher is giving him presents and sending him secret notes.

'OK,' he says. 'I know. But it will be tricky tonight. It's rather late.'

My instincts are screaming it's her.

'Nine o'clock *is* late in this house!' he says, laughing. 'I'm not a teenager any more.'

No, he's an adult. I wish he'd start acting like it. I've got to stop this affair with Miss Rotimi before Mum finds out. I cough loudly and then stomp into the room.

Dad looks up, and when he sees me he smiles. 'Anyway . . . my beautiful daughter has just walked in.'

He sounds calm. But is he faking it?

'I'll see what I can do,' he finishes. 'Bye. Speak soon.' He hangs up the phone and puts it in his pocket.

'Who was that?' I ask him, trying to sound casual.

'Just a friend,' he says. He turns away and puts the kettle on.

'What did she want?' I ask.

'Nothing,' he says. Then he frowns at me. 'How do you know it was a she? Were you eavesdropping?'

That's exactly what I was doing. I quickly change the subject.

'Do you know what *I* want?' I say.

'Hmm,' he says, getting out a teabag and a mug.

'One of your hot chocolates,' I tell him. I'm full from dinner but I'll suck down a sickly sweet hot chocolate if it means I can interrogate Dad. Subtly of course.

'What? *Now?*' he asks.

I nod and Dad rolls his eyes.

'Hey, Dad,' I say, pulling up a stool to sit at the breakfast bar while he gets the hot-chocolate stuff from the cupboard. Here goes. I can feel my heart rate rise. 'There's a new teacher at our school.'

'Hmm,' he says. He turns his back on me to get the milk out of the fridge.

'She's Nigerian,' I tell him.

'There are a few of us about,' he says.

'Her name is Miss Rotimi,' I say, and wait for a reaction. But I've mistimed it; his back is still to me. He reaches further into the fridge. 'I think her first name begins with I . . . or something.'

Dad spins round. He has a pained expression on his face.

'Do you want whipped cream on top?' he asks.

I sigh and try not to let it show. 'Um, yes, please,' I say. 'But this teacher—'

'Because I'm not sure we have any,' he says.

'Then why did you ask?' I throw my hands in the air dramatically.

Dad giggles. 'Sorry.'

'But Miss Rotimi,' I say again, getting more annoyed because I'm pretty sure he's avoiding my question, 'do you know her?'

Dad comes over to the counter and pours the milk into my favourite mug. 'You know what – I think I do,' he says.

He's admitted it. I'm not sure whether that's a good thing or a bad thing.

'There's a lady called Ife who goes to the jazz club from time to time,' he says. He puts the mug in the microwave so his back is to me again.

'What's she like?' I ask.

He shrugs. 'She's OK.'

He's not giving me anything. 'Some of the boys in our school think she's pretty.'

'Hmm.'

'What do *you* think?' I ask.

'I think those boys should be concentrating on their work rather than eyeing up the new teacher. Poor woman.'

'Dad!'

'What?' He frowns at me. 'What do you want me to say?'

I want him to say that Miss Rotimi is pretty but she's not his type. I want him to say that he loves Mum. Mum's gorgeous. And even though she's a bit moody at the moment there's no other woman in the world for him. Maybe if he admitted that he met up with Miss Rotimi and had a decent explanation as to why she gave him a record with a secret note in it, then everything would be OK again.

I want him to tell the truth. But only if it's the truth *I* want to hear.

'Nothing.' I jump down off the stool. 'It's just . . . I think she's ugly.' I charge out the room and back to the others.

I slump down next to Mum and sigh.

'You're very huffy today,' she says to me.

She noticed.

'Are you all right?'

'I'm fine.'

'You sound it,' she mutters.

Dad walks back into the TV room, holding my mug. Bem and Jumoke, like the sniffer dogs they are, notice straight away.

'What's that?' asks Bem. 'Can I have one?'

'Me too, please,' says Jumoke.

Dad smiles as he hands me my mug. 'See what you started?' he says. 'Darling,' he says to Mum, 'would you like a hot chocolate too?'

'No, thanks,' she says, not looking up. 'But a chamomile tea would be nice.'

'Coming right up,' he says. He turns and heads from the room and then turns right back again.

'Oh, and darling,' he says, 'I just got a call from one of my jazz pals. Turns out the club has got a great set of nights coming up over the next few weeks. You don't mind if I head along, do you?'

I look at Mum, wishing that she could read my mind. I want her to say that she wants to go with him – make a date out of it. I want her to show up at the jazz club and show Miss Rotimi that Dad has a wife who is just as beautiful as she is and she needs to back the hell off.

'Course not,' she says. 'Have fun.'

'You're not going to go too, Mum?' asks Bem. I could just kiss him right now. 'Get Dad to show you some of his moves?'

Mum wrinkles her nose. 'I've seen enough of his moves for a lifetime.'

'Blinking cheek!' Dad says as he moonwalks out again.

I look round at my family all smiling and laughing. I'm the only one who knows the truth. Well, Dad too of course: he's going to the club to meet up with Miss Rotimi.

I wonder how long this family's got before we're all broken apart.

Chapter 14

Donna's got everyone's attention. She's babbling away about something. And even though her arm is linked through mine, she hasn't noticed I'm not listening.

It's breaktime on Monday and all I've thought about the whole weekend is the idea my dad's having an affair with Miss Rotimi. I've been trying to come up with a way to stop it, everything from inserting a tracking device into his wallet to telling Mum what I know. But the thing is, I don't know *anything* for sure. And the only proof I had – the note she sent – I threw away.

Donna turns to me and I snap out of my thoughts. 'You will come with me, won't you?'

'Come with you *where*?' I ask.

Donna frowns. 'Have you not been listening to a word I've said?' she asks.

Hannah sniggers behind her hand.

I wince. 'I have a lot on my mind at the moment.'

Donna sighs, letting me off. But she doesn't ask me what the matter is.

'Great best friends you are,' Indiana whispers. Sonia scoffs.

'Are you OK, Obi?' Maxie asks me.

I open my mouth, then quickly close it again. If I follow Donna's advice, I shouldn't tell everyone every little detail of my problems. Should I talk it through with Donna later? One on one?

'I'm fine,' I say.

'Good,' says Donna. 'Because it's something about auditions.' She doesn't wait for me to reply. 'The audition for the solo singing part for the concert is on Wednesday at lunch. Will you come with me for moral support?'

'Of course,' I say. 'We all will. Won't we, girls? Us Boys' School Girls stick together like we promised.'

The others nod and hmm unenthusiastically.

'But you don't need it,' I tell Donna. 'You're

the best singer the school has.' This isn't me sucking up, this is just the truth. Donna has a voice like cupcake icing.

Donna beams at me. 'Aww, thanks,' she says, and nudges my arm. 'But it would really help if *you* were there supporting me. Miss Rotimi really likes you.'

Miss Rotimi. If I see that woman's face one more time . . . I've already decided: I'm not going to orchestra any more. I can't have her using me to pass any more notes. And if she comes to class again to ask me about it, I'll tell her I think her stupid orchestra is dumb. And that my dad thinks so too.

'Are you all right?' Donna asks. 'You just had a really sad expression on your face.'

She's finally noticed. She dips her chin low, looking concerned. I want to tell someone all about it. I want to confide in Donna – she says she's my best friend. Even though it doesn't feel like that yet, maybe if I tell her stuff it will make us closer. But then again, it was Donna herself who told me to keep things secret.

The girls are all looking at me.

'Obi?' says Maxie. 'What's up?'

I take a deep breath. But this is too big. Definitely too big to say in front of everyone.

'I just . . .' I chicken out and jump off the desk. 'I've just remembered I've left something in my locker.'

I run out of the room. What a wuss!

I don't go to my locker. And I don't want to hide in the girls' loos either – there's too much chance one of the others will walk in. Instead, even though it's cold, I head outside to the playground. Maybe a little icy air will freeze my brain and stop me thinking.

The boys are playing football as usual. I'm tempted to ask if I can join in. But I know the response – they'd look at me as if I were an alien. Us girls have been here less than a term. I'm pretty sure the boys aren't ready to allow a girl to play football, no matter how good I am.

Craig Hurst has the ball – he definitely wouldn't be ready.

I walk on past them. My plan is to just pace from the gate to the school and back again until break is finished.

'Obi!'

I'm smiling before I even turn round. 'Hi, Lenny,' I say. 'How are you?'

'Were you looking for me?' he asks. He's panting, just run off the pitch.

I wasn't looking for him. At least, I don't think I was.

'Er, not really, no,' I say.

'Oh.' He looks embarrassed, and maybe a little disappointed. 'How was your weekend? Did your brothers make it through without murdering each other?'

'They did,' I say, 'but my parents almost . . .'

'What?' he asks when I trail off.

'Nothing,' I say. If I can't tell the girls about my tragic family, there's no way I can tell him. There's an awkward pause.

'I'm going back to finish the game,' he says. 'But I'll see you at orchestra tonight, yeah?'

I shake my head. 'I'm not going.'

'What?! Why? You were the one who told me to do it, and now you're dropping out? I thought you said you loved music and anything was worth . . .'

I feel my lip starting to wobble so I bite it.

'Obi . . . what's up?' he asks.

'It's . . . I think . . .' But I can't say it out loud.

'What?' Lenny puts his hand on my upper arm. He has to bend down a bit so his eyes can meet mine. 'Tell me.'

And because I can't see a way out of telling him, or think up a decent lie, I say, 'I think there's something going on between Miss Rotimi and my dad.'

'Huh? What do you mean?'

I start pulling at the hair at the back of my neck. 'I mean . . . I think there's something *going on* between Miss Rotimi and my dad,' I repeat, begging him to get my meaning because I really don't want to spell it out properly.

He goes silent. Then, 'Why do you think that?'

I tell him everything. About the way Miss Rotimi knew all this stuff about me and my brothers. I don't say I'd hoped it was *him* that had told her. Then I tell him about the record, and the note. And the phone call. I don't know why, but I can't help it and it all just comes out. And he actually listens.

'The note said that she wanted to see him,' I say. 'That she wanted to see him *again*.'

Lenny rubs his cheek. 'Are you sure?' he says. 'Do you have the note now?'

I shake my head. 'I threw it away.' I cringe. What a stupid thing to do.

'I would've done the same,' he says, which makes me feel better.

'But look,' he says. 'Even if Miss Rotimi fancies your dad – and you don't know that for sure – it doesn't mean he likes her too. Your dad loves your mum . . .' he hesitates for a moment. 'Doesn't he?'

A massive lump forms in my throat. I realize I'm about to cry so I look away. 'All they do is fight.'

Lenny rubs his face again. He starts walking towards the school and brings me with him, not by touching me, but just by sticking by my side. 'Have you tried asking them about it?'

I shake my head. 'My family isn't really the talking kind.'

'Maybe you could change that.'

For some reason this makes me angry. 'Why should *I* be the one to talk? They're the adults. Why can't they just behave themselves?'

Lenny shrugs. 'They might be adults, but no one's perfect.'

I'm still angry, but not with Lenny. No one's perfect – I knew that. But I guess I always thought my parents were more together than most people. I guess I was wrong.

But what Lenny said *was* pretty perfect. If I want my mum and dad to stay together, I should do something about it. There's no point just watching, then crying when it all messes up.

Two seconds with Lenny and he's hit the nail on the head.

'Sounds like your mum's really busy, and she and your dad just need a little quality time together.'

'I suggested that exact thing to Mum,' I tell him. 'I told her she should go to the club. That way Miss Rotimi wouldn't be able to throw herself at him.'

'Good thinking! And what happened?' Lenny asks.

'She said she's not into jazz.'

'Oh.' He frowns hard. 'Well, don't give up. Why don't you and your brothers cook a meal for them? Make something nice and do the whole works – candles and everything.'

That's a pretty brilliant idea. Especially from a boy. I wouldn't mind doing all the cooking – I can't count on my brothers' help. But I've never done anything like this before. 'Wouldn't it be really obvious?'

Lenny shrugs. 'So what? If they see you're making an effort, hopefully it'll make them make the effort too.'

He's a twelve-year-old genius. 'I hope you're right,' I say. 'Thanks for helping me out with this.' And I step forward and give him a hug.

It's only when I'm snuggled up in his arms that I realize what I've done. It was the easiest thing in the world and I did it without thinking. And I really like it here. I wish I could hug him forever. But then the bell goes for the end of break.

We pull apart and it's a little embarrassing. Neither of us knows where to look.

'What do you have now?' I ask him quickly.

'Physics,' he says, and we both pull the same *yuck* face, then laugh.

'I've got French,' I say. 'I'll see you later.'

I go inside with the rest of the boys and head up the stairs. I'm in my own little dream world, thinking about what Lenny said, so I don't even notice when I walk smack into someone.

Sonia.

And from the look on her face I'm guessing she saw everything.

Chapter 15

'Sorry, Sonia, I didn't see you there,' I say.

She doesn't move, not an inch, and her glare is stuck on me.

'No, of course not,' she says. 'Don't let me get in your way. You just carry on.'

It doesn't take a genius to work out the double meaning in her words. Poor Sonia – publically dumped by Donna after following her around for so long. She must feel lonely. Just like I used to. I didn't mean to steal Donna from her – Donna labelled me as her best friend without even consulting me. But in Sonia's eyes, I stole Donna.

'Umm, thanks,' I say. 'I will.' Then I say. 'Look, I'm really sorry.'

Sonia flinches.

'I know Donna still likes you,' I tell her, even though Donna hasn't mentioned Sonia once. 'I think we just bonded the other day so she thinks of me as her new best friend.' Or at least, I think she does. I still don't know if our friendship is just a ploy to get to Lenny. But I don't tell Sonia this. 'You'll always be—'

Sonia tuts to interrupt me. She's hardened her face again. 'Oh please,' she says. 'Donna and I didn't know each other before we started at Hillcrest – we're hardly BFFs.'

'Hmm, I guess so.' Tara and Abby can fall out and make up again because they've been friends since they were four. But Sonia and Donna haven't covered the final *F* in BFF. Neither have me and Donna. I'm not sure we've even got to the *B* part.

'Do what you like,' Sonia says. 'Get tattoos of each other on your arms for all I care.'

I give a nervous laugh.

Then her face changes. She smiles. 'No hard feelings,' she says. But I'm not falling for it. 'In fact, I have something for you.'

'Oh yeah, what?'

She reaches out and grabs my hand. Then she pushes a piece of paper into it.

I look down and my heart suddenly flip-flops as I wonder if she's somehow got hold of Miss Rotimi's note to my dad.

'What's this?' I say with a nervous laugh. 'The code to a secret vault?'

'Much better than that,' she says.

I open it. It looks like a mobile number.

'It's Lenny's,' she says.

My heart flip-flops faster.

'Donna used to make me call him, pretending she wasn't there but she was listening in. She would write me a script about all the things I had to ask him. It was pretty pathetic.'

I should probably stick up for Donna – my best friend – but if it happened like Sonia said, then it does sound a little bit pathetic. 'So why are you giving it to me?' I ask.

'Because you need it,' she says.

I feel myself going red. 'Er . . . why exactly?'

'I saw you both just now.'

I close my eyes. I don't want to hear what she saw.

'I went to the loos, thinking you'd be there, and when you weren't I got suspicious and looked outside. What should I see? You and Lenny snogging each other's faces off.'

I laugh and cough at the same time. 'We weren't snogging!' I know I'm bright red now. 'He . . . did me a favour, that's all. I gave him a hug to say thanks.'

'Whatever, Obi,' she says, her eyes twinkling. 'I saw you.'

'But—'

'But,' she interrupts, 'let me just say that you should be slightly more subtle if you want to keep your relationship secret from you-know-who.'

'There is no relationship!' I protest.

'Not yet maybe,' says Sonia. 'But look – I'm going to help you. I'll make sure you get your man, and that Donna doesn't find out.'

I pass the piece of paper back to her, shaking my head. 'You're the one who told me about the Girl Code,' I remind her. 'I'm not going behind Donna's back.'

Sonia guffaws. 'Whatever,' she says again. 'But – ' she holds up a finger – 'there's something you should probably know about Donna.'

'Oh yeah,' I say. 'What's that?'

'She can't be trusted.' She puts both hands on her hips.

'That's a bit harsh, isn't it?' I say.

I want to defend my supposed new best friend, but Donna was Sonia's friend for way longer than she's been mine. She should know.

Sonia shakes her head. 'Not at all.' She's not finished. 'All the boasting she does, saying how great she is – it's all lies.'

'It's not all lies,' I point out. 'She boasts about her house and the way her parents spoil her. I've been to her house. It's true.'

Sonia rolls her eyes. 'Yeah, Princess Donna has the perfect life,' she says sarcastically.

'She does!' I say. 'I would give my house and family for a house and family half as cool as hers.'

Sonia shakes her head like she pities me. 'Believe what you want to believe,' she says. 'I did . . . at first. But Donna makes up half the stuff she says about herself.'

'Just because you're angry with her—'

'What about her little cinema trip with Lenny?' Sonia says.

OK, I know that wasn't true. 'She just got her dates confused,' I say. 'They got together on a different day.'

'She told us all they were going out,' says Sonia. 'But Lenny and Donna have never gone out.'

She's always implied they were boyfriend and girlfriend, but I don't remember her ever actually directly saying they were a proper couple. When I asked her about it, Donna told the truth and said they weren't.

Donna likes him – everyone knows – but if she's made up everything that she's said about him, she must really, *really* like him. Which means, if Donna and I have got any hope of becoming proper best friends, I've really, *really* got to stay away.

'I just thought I should warn you, that's all,' says Sonia, and she pushes her hair behind her shoulder.

'Warn me about *what*?' Now *I'm* getting a little annoyed with Sonia. I know Donna hurt her, but she's being really bitchy.

'I saw you copying her maths last week.'

'So?' Like Sonia's never cheated at school.

'Those answers she let you copy – they'll be wrong. All of them. She'll tell you it was a joke and you'll laugh it off.'

'Don't be stupid—'

Sonia throws her hands in the air. 'She did the same to me.'

'What a load of bull.' I've had enough of Sonia's stirring.

'Let's prove it, shall we?'

Sonia virtually drags me over to the staff room and knocks on the door.

'Sonia,' I say, 'what are you . . .'

The door opens.

'Can I help you, girls?' asks Mrs Bartlet.

Sonia smiles sweetly and bats her eyelids. 'Is Mrs Grabovski there, please?' she asks. 'We have a question about maths.'

Mrs Bartlet disappears inside and we wait. I cross my arms in front of my chest – this is such a waste of time. But then I look at how smug Sonia seems and it makes me nervous.

Mrs Grabovski comes to the door, and when

she sees it's me she frowns. 'Obi,' she says. 'Just the girl I was after.'

Now I'm *really* nervous. 'Oh?'

'I need to talk to you about the work we did in class last week. Your simultaneous equations weren't just wrong, they were way off. It was as if you plucked the numbers out of nowhere.'

My heart sinks. Sonia was right. Donna set me up.

'Would you like to explain yourself?' asks Mrs Grabovski.

How would I explain all this? 'Umm . . . I just . . . it was too hard.' I hang my head.

Mrs Grabovski isn't buying it. 'Then come to see me after school today and we'll go through it again.'

My mouth falls open. Sonia looks at me, her eyebrows raised in an I-told-you-so gesture.

'Three thirty in the library,' says Mrs Grabovski. 'I'll see you there.' She closes the door on me.

Great! Now I have detention. I'll have to come up with another story for Mum and Dad about why I'm late home again.

Sonia rounds on me. 'See! Told you she couldn't be trusted!'

Sonia was right. Suddenly everything I thought about my friendship with Donna has been thrown out the window. I knew I should have trusted my instincts. The reason we didn't feel like best friends is because we *weren't* best friends. Best friends don't do this kind of thing to each other.

'And there's something else you should know,' says Donna.

'Yeah? What?' I'm angry, but not with Sonia.

'I've got physics next,' Sonia continues. 'With Lenny.'

'And?' I ask. Where's she going with this?

'And you have his number,' she says, pressing the piece of paper into my hand again. 'Only fair I give him yours.'

'Umm . . .'

'See you later, lover-girl,' she says to me, and she wiggles her eyebrows then heads back down the stairs again. I did't tell her to give Lenny my number, but I didn't tell her not to either.

I'm not sure how Donna's going to explain what she did to me, but I feel much less guilty about talking to Lenny now.

Secret meet-ups and secret notes. I get a wiggly feeling in my tummy. I'm nervous. But I'm also excited. I wonder if he'll call me.

Chapter 16

On Tuesday I'm walking down the corridor towards the dining hall to meet the girls when a piece of paper hits me on the back of the head.

I look round for the culprit, expecting it to be one of my idiotic brothers, but I can't see anyone.

I start walking again. Then fly off my feet as I'm yanked sideways into a classroom.

'Ow!' I say, now certain it's one of my brothers. Only they would—

But when I look up it's Sonia, her ginger hair coming out of her ponytail in strands.

'Oh,' I say. 'It's you.' I soften a little. 'That hurt.' I rub my arm where she grabbed me.

'Sorry,' she says, wearing a cheeky grin.

She doesn't look that sorry.

'But when you see where we're going, you'll be pleased I grabbed you.'

What's she got up her sleeve this time? 'Where are you taking me?'

'Not where,' she says, wiggling her eyebrows. '*Who*.'

'OK . . . *who*?' I ask. But I can guess the answer.

'Lenny of course!' she says, and clasps her hands together.

Of course. I didn't have to wait long to hear from Lenny. He texted me as soon as class finished, and we've been messaging ever since.

Donna and I talk at school and text every night too, but never about anything personal: just hair or music or whatever. I didn't tell her about talking to Lenny, but then she never gave me the chance. Is not telling the same as lying?

'What are you scheming?' I definitely don't trust Sonia. She totally has a reason for wanting to stitch me up.

Sonia puts her hands to her chest all innocently. 'Nothing.' Then she laughs. 'OK, not nothing. I'm playing cupid. Lenny asked me to ask you to come and meet him in music room 4. He told me to drag you by your hair if that's what it takes. He wants to *practise* with you.' She wiggles her eyebrows again. 'And who knows what that means?'

I feel as wiggly as Sonia's eyebrows. I don't know if I like Lenny like that. But I do like the fact he wants to meet up with me.

Sonia grabs my arm and pulls me out of the room, but not before checking both ways down the corridor. 'Come on,' she says. 'Before it gets back to Donna.'

We're running, and my accelerating heartbeat is not helping to reduce the excitement.

'But what about Donna?' I say, panting. 'She'll notice if I don't turn up to lunch.'

'Oh yeah,' she says, 'your best friend.' I can hear the sarcasm in her voice. 'Don't worry about that. I'll cover for you.'

I'm not so sure.

'I'll say you had to stay late in History,' she says.

We run down the stairs to the basement where the small music rooms are.

'Why would you do that for me?' I ask. 'I thought you hated me.'

153

Sonia stops and looks me in the eye. 'I don't hate *you*,' she says. 'I hate her. You're just her next victim. If anything, I feel sorry for you.'

I gulp and pull at the hair at the back of my neck. Deep down I've been wondering if this is true – that I'm being used just like Sonia was.

'Lenny likes you,' says Sonia. 'Much more than he ever liked Donna. If I can help you get together, it would make me happy. The Boys' School Girls helping each other out and all that.'

I don't believe a word of it.

'And if it brings Donna down a peg or two at the same time, then what an added bonus!'

Now *that* I believe.

'But . . .'

'What?'

'But I care about Donna's feelings, even if you don't,' I say, my conscience finally catching up with me.

Sonia starts smoothing back my hair with her hands. 'What she doesn't know won't hurt her.'

This was Miss Rotimi's line. I'm not sure if I like it any more.

Sonia gets out some lipgloss and starts aiming for my mouth. I yank my head away.

'Fine!' says Sonia. 'You look lovely as you are.'

I'm in the middle of scoffing at her for that comment when she spins me round, opens the door to room 4 and pushes me inside.

I stumble forward and fall straight into Lenny. He catches me just in time.

'Oh! Hi!' he says. 'A hell of an entrance.'

'Umm.' I can feel myself blushing. 'Yes. I . . . er . . .' I look back at Sonia, who's smirking in the doorway.

'Thanks for doing that for me, Sonia,' he says.

'Any time, Lenny.' She winks, then closes the door behind her. 'You lovebirds have fun now.'

I rub my arm at the spot where Sonia grabbed me. 'You know, you could have just messaged me,' I say. 'It would have been a lot less painful.'

He laughs. 'Yeah, but then how would I know you'd actually come? Say what you like about Sonia, she gets the job done.'

I have to laugh at that.

'You're probably wondering why you're here,' he says.

I nod.

'Did Donna tell you about the party on Saturday?' he asks me.

I frown. She didn't. If not telling *is* the same as lying, then Donna's pants are on fire. I shake my head. 'What party?' I ask.

'Some girl that Donna used to know from her old school,' he says. 'She wants Sucker Punch to play.'

'That's cool,' I say unenthusiastically. My mind is reeling with all the things Donna's kept from me. I feel stupid for thinking we were friends. Why didn't I trust my instincts?

'You have to come,' he says to me. 'You have to play with us.'

'Mum will never let me go to a party of a girl I don't know. Especially not to play in a band.' I feel so low. Not only has Donna kept this party from me but Sucker Punch will be performing and I can't perform with them.

Lenny takes both my hands. 'So don't tell her,' he says with a grin. 'Don't mention the band bit.'

I shake Lenny off, too moody to grin back at him. 'I don't know enough of your stuff.'

'That's why you're here. To practise,' he says. He turns to me and looks me in the eye. 'Me and you.'

I can feel myself blushing.

'We'll do it at break and lunch so you don't have to tell your mum and dad.'

I'm so glad he understands the deal with my parents without me having to explain.

'I'll get you up to speed,' he says. 'All you have to do is get yourself to this party on Saturday.'

I smile. I would love to play at my first gig. This isn't just to do with Lenny, it's to do with how much I love music. If I'm not going to be in orchestra, I must play with them. And if I can persuade Sucker Punch to have a big-band influence . . .

'Umm . . . OK,' I say. 'Why not?' It will show Donna she can't control me. I can't wait to see her face when I turn up with my trumpet on Saturday.

'So. You ready?' he asks, picking up his guitar.

'Nope,' I say. 'I don't have my trumpet.'

'I borrowed one,' he says.

I put my hand up to refuse. I'm not playing Miss Rotimi's trumpet.

'Before you ask, it wasn't from her. I borrowed it from Vincent Chen. I owe him a look at my biology homework.'

I smile. That was really nice of Lenny to guess I would feel that way about Miss Rotimi's stuff. I pick up the trumpet and examine it. It's more expensive than mine, but not as shiny.

Lenny hands me a piece of music. 'OK, let me talk you through this first one — it's called *Brain Drain*. It's about how Joel feels about revision.'

I squint at the sheet. It's handwritten and has been photocopied a few times so it's hard to read.

'Can't we start with something easier?' I ask. 'Something legible?'

'Ha!' he guffaws.

'Or at least something I know?' I flip the paper back and forth. 'Don't you guys do any covers?'

Lenny winces. 'Not really,' he says. 'Thing is, Joel only wants to play our music – exclusively. Reece is pretty easy-going, but he prefers that too – he says cover bands only get hired for weddings, not the Introducing Stage at Glastonbury.'

'What do you think?' I ask.

'I just want to please the crowd,' he says. 'Isn't that what music is all about? Surely it's supposed to be for the listeners, not the musicians.'

I think about it for a second. 'Ideally it should be both. If the band's enjoying what they're playing, I reckon you can hear it in the sound. It depends on the mood of the musicians, how they're feeling, how they're getting on with each other. That's why live music is so special – it's never the same – like a snowflake! There's a kind of energy when you hear music played live because . . .'

I trail off. Lenny's looking at me weirdly.

'I'm babbling, aren't I?' I say.

He nods and grins. 'A little.'

I feel hot.

'It's cute.'

I feel hotter.

'You're cute,' he says. His look has gone all intense and he steps towards me. It's like he's going to kiss me. I step back. My first thought — annoyingly — is Donna. Even though I'm not sure about her, I can't help but feel bad.

'What about Donna?' I ask.

'Donna will sing anything that makes her voice sound good — which is anything,' he replies. 'So she doesn't mind what we perform.'

Lenny thought I was talking about music.

'I mean,' I say, 'is there anything going on with you and Donna?'

'I've told you before,' he says. 'No.'

'But how come you two are so close?' I ask, amazed that I'm being so open with him. If I don't think about it, it seems the honesty just slips out.

'Donna . . .' Lenny looks to the ceiling. 'Well, you know we live near to each other,' he says, looking back at me. 'And obviously we're band mates. We just got close. People think Donna's one way, but actually she's not like that at all.'

'Really?' I ask. This makes me feel better. I want to believe Donna is a good person because I want to feel like we're best friends for real.

Lenny nods. 'Donna has her – you know – certain, erm, *behavioural issues*. And she has her secrets. But she's a nice girl deep down.'

I know about Donna's behavioural issues, and I've figured out by now about her hiding stuff. But if she's hiding things from me, how are we really best friends?

'So if you think I'm not single,' Lenny says, 'I am. Completely and one hundred per cent single.' I can see his cheeks reddening. 'In case you wanted to know.' He turns away from me. 'For any reason.'

Now my cheeks are burning. I have nothing to say and the awkwardness fills the air like an out-of-tune note in a music exam.

I clear my throat. 'Do you think I'll be

ready for Saturday? I'm not just going to come and stand onstage with my trumpet like a melon.'

Lenny laughs. 'I think the expression is *like a lemon*.'

'Does it really matter?' I reply. 'I'll look like a fruit either way!'

'That's why you're here now,' he says.

'Why else would I be here?'

I pretend it's about the music, and of course it is a bit. Music missing from my life makes me feel like someone's shaved my hair off. But there could be another reason why I'm here – the sneaking around. The wiggly feeling in my stomach. Am I really here just to spend time with Lenny?

'Actually we do do one cover,' he says. '*Valerie*, the Amy Winehouse version. Do you know it?'

When I nod he picks up his guitar. I put the trumpet to my lips and we both start to play. With the music surrounding us, this is the most relaxed I've felt in a long time. I want to think it's because of the song we're playing, and not because of the gorgeous boy I'm standing next to.

Chapter 17

I'm with Tara, Abby and Candy and we push open the door to the girls' loos.

'Yoohoo!' I shout. 'Miss Donna Woods. It's your curtain call in five.'

We giggle.

'I'm coming,' Donna calls back over a cubicle door.

'Come on,' Abby adds. 'We don't want to keep the judges waiting. Who knows – Miss Rotimi might have called in Simon Cowell.'

We giggle again. Even though just hearing Miss Rotimi's name makes my skin crawl, I try to laugh it off. My dad has stayed in every night since Saturday so I'm confident nothing's happened. Not since then at least. But how long before Miss Rotimi uses her charms to get him out of the house and into her spider's web?

Donna flings open the cubicle door and

pushes it back with her whole arm. She leans against the door frame and puts her hand up to her forehead dramatically. 'Well, in that case . . .' she says, looking at us and batting her eyelids.

'Oh dear, we've got ourselves a diva already,' I say.

'Already?' says Tara. 'Donna was *born* a diva.' Even though Donna and Tara haven't always got on, everyone knows Tara's teasing. Us girls might have our ups and downs, but we made a promise to stick together when times are tough. And that's what I'm doing now – I'm still mad at Donna about the maths, and not telling me about the party, but spending all this time with Lenny behind her back is pretty bad too. I guess that makes us even.

'Come on,' I say to her. 'The auditions have already started.'

'Give me five more minutes,' she says.

Tara rolls her eyes.

'Mind if we meet you there?' asks Abby. 'Joel is trying out too and I don't want to miss it.'

Donna waves us away. 'Sure,' she says.

I head out with the rest of them but Donna calls me back. 'Obi Wan,' she says, 'will you wait with me?'

I hesitate and she must have caught it because she adds, 'Please?'

I look down at my phone. Lenny texted me earlier, asking me to meet him in one of the music rooms again. But I have a few minutes.

'Sure,' I say. 'What's up?'

She shrugs. 'Nothing.'

So why do I have to wait with you? I think.

'I've been feeling guilty about something,' she says. 'And I want to apologize.'

I think I know what she's going to say. 'Is this about the maths?'

She scrunches up her face and nods. 'I'm sorry I gave you the wrong answers. It was a joke.'

This is what Sonia said she'd say.

'Not a very funny one,' I tell her. At least we're *starting* to be real with each other.

'I know,' she says. 'I don't even know why I did it.'

'Mrs Grabovski gave me a detention,' I say crossly.

Donna shakes her head at her own actions. 'Sometimes I'm a cow for no reason. I hate myself for it. A therapist would have a field day with me.'

'A field *week*,' I mutter.

Donna snorts. Then she softens again. 'But I really am sorry.'

For some reason my instinct says to believe her. And as I'm guilty of lying to her too, I decide to let it go.

'That's OK,' I say.

'Still best friends?' she asks.

I nod, even though it's not true and I'm not sure it ever has been. But that apology felt like the most sincere thing that's ever passed between us. My meet-ups with Lenny burn a little. I'm not sure how long I can convince myself that *what she doesn't know won't hurt her* is OK.

Donna gets her make-up bag out. Then she unzips it and gets out her mascara. 'Just a lick of mascara,' she says. 'For luck.'

'You don't need it,' I say. 'You're a great singer.'

'Aww, thanks.'

'And none of the rest of us are auditioning anyway!' I lighten my voice. 'When it comes to the female solo, you literally have no competition!'

Donna smiles. 'You guys are the best.'

This is what I mean about us girls sticking together. I don't think you'd catch the boys doing that.

'Lenny's not auditioning,' she says.

I knew that already. He told me there was no way he was putting himself front of stage.

'We planned it together yesterday,' says Donna.

So Lenny spoke to her about it too. 'Oh yeah?'

'We were both going to audition, but then I said it wouldn't be good if we became one of those celebrity couples who were always competing with each other to be the more famous one. He's going to leave the singing to me.'

When I spoke to him he didn't say anything

about the celebrity-couple stuff. Must be another one of Donna's lies.

'Would you do this for me, please?' she asks.

She's got her mascara up by her eyelashes and her hands are shaking.

'You're not nervous, are you?' I ask. 'You know you're going to get the part.'

She smiles weakly. 'I think I probably am. But that makes it worse. What if I mess it up? What if my voice suddenly decides to disappear?

I laugh. 'What if you pee yourself in front of everyone?'

She's not laughing. 'I'm serious, Obi. I get really bad stage fright.'

'Please, you're a natural . . .' I look at her to see if she's lying now, like she's lied about so much. But then it all starts to make sense – why she was hiding in the toilets. Why she sent the other girls from the room, but asked me to stay: she's scared.

'I just pretend to be a natural,' she says. 'It's all fake.'

I walk over to her, take the mascara from

her hands and start applying it gently to her lashes. 'I had no idea.'

'No one does. I don't want people to think I'm weird.'

So she does follow her own advice about telling everyone everything.

'You're not weird,' I say. 'In fact, you'd be weird if you *weren't* nervous.'

'There's a lot people don't know about me,' she says. Her lips start to tremble. 'In fact . . .' She shakes her head. Can those be tears in her eyes? 'Never mind.'

'Tell me.' I don't want to get sucked in again, but suddenly I'm starting to think there's some deep issue that makes her act the way she does.

Donna smiles her supermodel smile. 'I'm fine. It's silly.'

And now I realize she uses that smile when she's lying. All this time I thought she talked too much, but she talks a lot to hide her real self. If she's not ready to open up, then I won't push her. I just have to make sure I'm here when she *is* ready.

'OK,' I say.

'Thanks, Obi.'

'No problem.'

'I know you said you can't come to watch the auditions, but I'd really appreciate it if you *were* there. For me. Your best friend.'

I told her I had homework, when really me and Lenny are meeting up. I don't want to be in the same room as Miss Rotimi — I hate her guts — and I know she'll ask me why I haven't been to orchestra all week.

But Donna needs me. And just now I saw a glimmer of something that could be a real friendship. Donna might be the best friend I'm after, after all. I'd be stupid — and mean — not to do this one nice thing for her.

I hand Donna back her mascara and send Lenny a quick text:

> *Going to the auditions. Donna needs the moral support. We can practise later x*

I end all my texts to Lenny with kisses now. He started it.

Spoilsport ☺ *OK I'll come find you x*

'Who's that?' asks Donna.

'Nothing,' I say. 'No one.'

I drop my phone back in my bag. Luckily Donna is too busy applying lipgloss to ask any more. Now that I've forgiven her for the maths thing, and I'm allowing her to be my best friend, lying to her about Lenny is going to be a whole lot harder.

Chapter 18

If Miss Rotimi has picked up that I'm scowling at her, she hasn't let it show. She's wearing a bright pink dress which is way too short and tarty for school.

'Come on, ladies,' she says. 'You're all here. One of you might as well audition too.'

She looks around at us. But Donna has just sung, and sung brilliantly. I knew she was nervous, but only because she told me. Her voice sounded really, really good as she sang a beautiful Sarah McLachlan song.

Me and the other girls exchange looks, all shaking our heads. We're here for Donna, not to sing.

'Come on,' she says. 'Just one of you.'

Her eyes fall on me. She smiles. Can't she sense how much I hate her?

'Obi . . . ?'

I don't answer.

'How about it?' she finishes.

'No, thanks,' I say.

'No?' she says. She steps forward and takes me by the arm. 'I bet you have a great voice. Why don't you sing?'

I stare down at the place where she has a hold of my arm like she's causing me pain. She lets go.

'Come on . . .' she coaxes. Then she turns to the rest of the room. 'Come on, everyone. Don't you want to hear Obi sing?'

She claps her hands together and starts chanting. The girls look at each other and one by one they join in. Miss Rotimi has made cajoling me into a fun game and they've all been taken in by it.

'*O-bi. O-bi. O-bi.*'

Have they completely forgotten that we told Donna that we wouldn't?

'Come on, Obi,' Miss Rotimi simpers. 'Show me what you can do. We've got the music to *Silent Night* up on the stand.'

'Fine,' I say, and haul myself up. I'll show

her what I can do. 'You've asked for it.' She can't wrap me round her finger like she does everyone else.

I get to the middle of the room where the music stand is. Donna gives me a worried look, but I wink at her and she relaxes.

I start singing *Silent Night*, as instructed. But I use my best Donald Duck voice to do it.

'♫ *Silent night* ♫' I quack.

People start sniggering. I'm partly doing this to get at Miss Rotimi and also to show Donna that we're friends.

'♫ *Holy night. (Quack quack.)* ♫'

Everyone's laughing now. I see Sonia take out her phone and start pressing it. I hope she's not recording me.

'♫ *All is quack* ♫'

Miss Rotimi's face falls into a dark frown as

174

she looks at me. 'OK, OK,' she says, her hands raised. 'Very funny. Now sing it properly please, Obi.'

'But I don't want to,' I tell her.

Miss Rotimi sighs. She realizes she's up against a conspiracy — the Boys' School Girls want Donna to get the part, and we'll do whatever we can to make it happen.

'I can't persuade you to try?' she pleads.

I shake my head.

'I'll do it,' comes a voice I know well. When did Lenny get here? He's over by the door and he pushes through the people sitting around the room and comes to the middle to join me.

'Sonia just texted me to say you were singing,' he whispers. 'I happened to be passing . . .'

Sonia's grinning. She wasn't recording me.

'Come on, Obi,' Lenny says a little louder. 'We'll sing together.'

My mouth has fallen open so I quickly shut it.

I look at Donna. Her face is frozen. I've just stolen her limelight. However great her singing was — and it was amazing — I've just made everyone laugh, and now I'm being heroically rescued by the fittest boy in the year.

Donna gives me a thumbs-up. She wants me to do well. I guess she *is* my real friend after all. I feel pretty bad.

'I'm not going to give up until you do,' Miss Rotimi says, batting her eyelashes.

Then Lenny's beside me and I feel better.

'You ready?' he whispers.

Everyone's eyes are on me and I feel the pressure. I don't want to – even if it wasn't for Miss Rotimi, I'm not used to being the centre of attention.

But with Lenny by my side it makes it easier.

I nod and look into his eyes. 'Ready.'

'Donald Duck or normal?' he asks with a grin.

I can't help but smile.

Miss Rotimi sits at her piano, looking very pleased with herself. Then she starts up the music.

'♫ *Silent night, holy night* ♫'

We're singing together, for real this time. I didn't realize that Lenny had such a good voice. Mine's OK – I'm holding my own and everything – but Lenny's is the one that shines through.

'♫ *All is calm, all is bright* ♫'

All eyes are on us. But then I see they aren't looking at me at all – they're all hooked on Lenny, even Tara, and she's so madly in love with Reece it's not true.

'♫ *Round yon Virgin Mother and Child* ♫'

Some idiots giggle at the word *virgin*.

'♫ *Holy infant so tender and mild* ♫'

The fact that all the focus is on me, but also not really on *me*, gives me confidence. I can sing as loudly as I want and no one will really notice.

Here comes the high bit. I'm going for it.

'♫ *Sleep in heavenly pee-eace* ♫'

We're nailing this song. It feels just as good as when I'm nailing one of my trumpet pieces. I grin up at him and he grins right back.

' ♫ *Sleep in heavenly peace* ♫ '

Then he adds a silly flourish to the end and everyone laughs again. Then applauds.

Donna jumps up and runs over to us. She hugs Lenny first, then me. 'That was great, guys,' she says. 'Really good.'

I beam back at her, so glad she's not annoyed with me. 'Nowhere near as good as you. But at least I didn't embarrass myself.'

'I don't know,' says Sonia, who has appeared beside Donna. 'I think Obi's a real contender for that solo part.' Then she looks at Lenny. 'You two have natural chemistry. Have you been practising together?'

My heart lurches and I begin to panic. Sonia knows about our secret meet-ups. She's just been waiting for the right moment to break it to Donna.

Donna narrows her eyes at Sonia. Then she

turns to me. 'I'd have practised with you. Given you some tips.'

Before I would have taken this as a veiled insult. And it still sort of is, but now I know Donna a little better I can see that it's covering up something else — something bigger. Donna is terrified of me stealing Lenny away from her. And worse still, people finding out about it.

'I didn't know you could sing, Obi,' says Indiana.

'I can't,' I say, holding my hands up.

'With a little more practice,' says Abby, 'you could be excellent.'

'Obi and Lenny are made for each other.' Sonia looks pointedly at Donna. '*Musically*, I mean.'

I have to stop her before she says any more. I shake my head. 'This is never happening again. Do you know what it took for me to sing up there?'

'It took Lenny,' says Sonia, raising her eyebrows.

Candy giggles.

I ignore them. 'My legs are shaking. My palms are covered in sweat. I feel like I might be sick. All this – ' I point to the podium – 'it's just not worth it.'

Donna holds my hand. 'It doesn't come naturally for everyone.'

About fifteen minutes ago she said it didn't come naturally for her. Was she lying when she said that? Or, is it what I think it is and Donna isn't as confident as she makes out?

'You did great.' It's Miss Rotimi. We all turn around to look at her. 'Really great. I'm sorry I forced you into it,' she says. 'But see the results! Two new stars in the making!'

Now Donna's face looks like thunder.

'Well done, Obi.' Miss Rotimi pats me on the shoulder and I jerk away.

'Can I go now?' I growl at her.

Miss Rotimi's smile falters for a second, then she nods. 'Of course.'

I head out of there. The other girls follow behind me, already chatting away. 'I still think Donna will get it,' says Hannah. 'But maybe Miss Rotimi will make Obi her understudy.'

'Thank you for the opportunity, Miss Rotimi!' calls Donna, like an auditionee on a talent show. 'Do you need any help packing things away?'

Donna thinks she has to suck up to help her chances at getting the part. She's more insecure than I thought. Either that or she actually likes Miss Rotimi. I need to tell Donna that Miss Rotimi is not the cool person we thought she was. I'm disgusted that I used to think that way about her.

I get outside the door and stride on ahead. I want to be as far away from that woman as possible.

'Hey, partner.' Lenny's next to me again. 'Any chance you could play the trumpet and sing at the same time?'

He makes me laugh. Despite my foul mood. 'That'd be some feat.'

He whispers in my ear. 'Come and meet me tomorrow. We'll practise again. Maybe think about getting in some harmonies.'

I give him a look that says, *Are you crazy?*

'Are you crazy?' I say out loud, in case he

didn't get the message from my glare. 'You know Donna won't go for that.'

'I don't see why not,' he says. 'She'd still be the star of the show – you would just be enhancing her voice.'

I turn back and see Sonia right behind us. I blush because she's caught us whispering into each other's ears. She raises her eyebrows. 'Don't mind me,' she says and passes us by.

'Here's the deal,' I say. 'I'll do the trumpet. But I'm not singing.'

'But—'

'Either I'm not singing, or I'm not coming. Get it?'

Lenny stands up straight and salutes. 'Loud and clear, captain.'

I giggle.

'Tomorrow at lunch?' he asks.

I look back for Donna, unsure of how I feel about her. Meeting up with Lenny again would be a real betrayal of our friendship. Especially as I'm starting to think it *is* a real friendship.

But now that I'm not in orchestra, Sucker Punch is my only chance to be in a band. What if Donna's not a real friend and I'm missing out to be loyal to someone who doesn't deserve my loyalty?

Should I betray Donna for Lenny?

Chapter 19

I hear a noise downstairs. I put my trumpet on my bed.

Mum has her polite voice on — a little higher than normal and she's speaking really fast. 'No, no, it's no problem at all,' she says. But the squeakiness implies that there *is* a problem in actual fact.

'I won't be long, I promise, Mrs Udogu,' replies the visitor.

It's Donna.

'I just wanted to give Obi . . . some . . . homework,' she says.

'Well, that's fine then.' The ogre can't refuse entry when someone utters the magic 'homework' password.

When I get to the top of the stairs I see my whole family gazing at Donna like Mum just let a panda into our house. Excited that this is something new, but also a bit nervous. Bem's just in his boxers so he's really embarrassed.

'Can I get you a drink?' Dad asks, peering out from the kitchen. 'A Coke or something?'

Donna looks up and sees me on the landing. She grins.

'No, thank you,' she says. 'I won't be—'

'Thanks, Dad,' I yell, 'but no thanks. Come up, Donna!'

I haven't had a friend over for ages. Definitely not since I started Hillcrest. My room is so small – nothing compared to Donna's. And I have all my big-band-music stuff lying around. What if she laughs at it? What if she calls me 'lame'?

Still, it's better she's in my room than that she spends too much time with my nightmare family. As Donna climbs on up, trying not to giggle at Bem in his boxers, I can already hear Mum muttering to Dad, 'Are you sure we should allow this?'

'Oh, let the girl have some fun,' Dad says.

'That's your attitude to everything—'

I pull Donna into my bedroom and slam the door behind her so she can't hear any more of their bickering.

'Hi! What are you doing here? It's so good to see you,' I say, and I realize that I'm sounding a little like my mum a moment ago. I hurriedly stack up the sheets of music, hoping she won't ask about them. 'How come you didn't say you were coming round?'

'Surprise!' she says. Then she grimaces. 'Is that OK? Aren't you allowed people over? I'm sorry if I made your mum angry. I should have checked.'

I sigh. 'You didn't make her angry. She's pretty much always angry these days.'

'Is everything all right?' Donna asks.

I plonk myself down on my bed. 'Sometimes I wonder if it would be easier if they did get divorced. It would certainly be less shouty round here.'

Donna sits next to me and puts her arm around me. 'Shouting is bad,' she says. 'But silences are worse.'

'I know!' I say. 'Sometimes I have to run up

here and play my trumpet just to check I haven't gone deaf!'

Donna gives a sad laugh. 'Nothing like belting out *My Heart Will Go On* to drown the silences in my house.'

'At least the silences in your house are just because your Dad's working away,' I say. 'I'm sure you miss him and everything, but . . .'

Donna sniffs. She's not crying, is she? She wouldn't cry over my problems, would she? Maybe best friends do that.

'Yeah,' she says. 'He works away a lot.'

'But when my parents break up it won't be that he's off for a few days; he'll be gone for good.' Then I think about how much time Mum spends at home compared to Dad. She's hardly ever here because she's always at the office. 'Actually, Dad might get the house and Mum might move out. But I wonder if that happens when Dad's the one who's . . .'

I feel a lump in my throat and stop myself telling Donna about my dad's affair with Miss Rotimi, a) because I don't know for sure if it's happening, and b) because I don't know if I can trust her. When I look back at Donna she's wiping her eyes.

'Sorry,' I say. 'I'm upsetting you. I've been trying to follow your advice about not telling everyone everything, and here I am babbling away about my problems, making you sad for me. It's OK,' I tell her. 'We'll be all right.'

'Of course you will,' she says, pulling herself up straight and sticking her nose in the air. 'We're survivors.'

Though I don't know what she has to survive.

'Quick thinking, telling Mum you had homework to give me,' I say. 'You're a good liar.' Oops! I meant it as a compliment, but maybe she'll be offended.

'I *am* a good liar,' she boasts.

Apparently not.

'But it was only half a lie. I do have something for you . . . A present.'

A random present. Not for my birthday or Christmas or anything. This is definitely best-friend behaviour.

She pulls her bag on to her lap and opens it.

Then she pulls out a CD. 'Do you have a CD player?' she asks.

'There's one downstairs,' I say.

On the front of the album is an old man holding an oboe. I recognize him instantly. 'Benny Goodman!' I say, and grab the CD from her. 'Cool!'

'Well, I remembered you talking about him,' she says. 'Then I found this in my mum's music collection and gave it a listen.'

I wince. It was in her mum's music collection – does that mean she automatically thinks it's uncool? But when I look at Donna's face her eyes are wide and excited.

'It's great!' she says. 'I can see why you like it so much!'

'Really?' I ask.

'Yes! I listened to the whole album. Twice. We absolutely need to incorporate some of this stuff into Sucker Punch's sound.'

I haven't felt this happy in a long time. Not only has Donna got me a present, but it's something she knew I'd like. And she even listened to the album.

'Why don't we make notes about places we could add in your trumpet into our songs?' She's looking round the room for a pen. 'I've brought some of our stuff . . .'

I hope she doesn't see the sheet with the music to *Brain Drain* written out. She'd know Lenny gave it to me. And she'd guess that we've been meeting up in secret.

'Do you know our song *Ballistic*? I was thinking you could come in just after the first verse when it starts to get more intense . . .' She carries on talking but I'm just watching her, amazed. It hits me. She's a really, really good friend now. She might even actually be my *best* friend.

'Then after the second chorus . . . what?' she says. She's noticed me staring. She runs over to the mirror to check her face. 'Have I got something on me?'

'No! Nothing,' I say. 'Just . . . thanks for this, Donna.'

She shrugs. 'That's what best friends are for.'

I hesitate for a minute. 'Is that what we are?' I ask. 'Really?'

Donna sits back down next to me again. 'I admit,' she says, 'at first I did befriend you because I thought you could give me the inside track to Lenny's mind. I thought you might even be competition.'

I gulp. Lenny. She has no idea.

'But then I got to know you,' she says. 'You'd never do that. Not to another girl, and not to me. You're too loyal.'

I feel a bit sick. I've been disloyal and kept secrets while saying she's my best friend. Who have I become?

'You and me are different, Obi Wan,' she says, 'but opposites attract.' She smiles, showing her teeth. Her genuine smile.

All this time I wanted a best friend. I finally found one in Donna and I've been keeping secrets from the very beginning. Not actually lying, but not telling her the truth, and that's just as bad.

'We might have nothing in common,' she says, 'but who cares?'

'We don't have *nothing* in common,' I remind her. 'We have music and . . .' I scour my mind for anything else, 'and maybe that's it.'

'Ha!' Donna bursts out laughing. 'And talking of music,' she says, 'what are you doing tomorrow night?'

Here it is. She's finally telling me about the gig.

'Umm,' I say. 'Nothing.' If I admit that I already know about it, but then she'll ask how I know, and then I'll have to tell her about me and Lenny. I don't want to ruin our best-friendship when it's only just started.

'Good,' she says, 'because we have a gig!'

I know.

'Well, it's not a proper gig really,' she says. 'It's just my old friend Harriet's party. But we'll be playing and there will be people listening, so we're calling it a gig.'

'Umm.' I don't know if I can do this. I do so want to play with Sucker Punch, play in front of people. But there's the Lenny complication. And another one that's much more obvious. 'You've seen what my mum's like. I'm not sure she'll let me.'

'So ask your dad!' she says.

'And risk the outbreak of war?' I ask.

Donna does a big pout. 'But I wanted us to get ready together. I was going to straighten your hair again.'

'I'll see if I can persuade them,' I say.

'Make sure you do,' she leans in close and whispers to me, 'because I need your help.'

'Oh yeah?'

'I want to try and get Lenny alone. I'm hoping we might kiss.'

I gulp. So this is my mission: help Donna and Lenny get together. The trouble is, I think that's going to be really hard. I don't think Lenny fancies Donna – no matter how badly she wants him to.

Because . . . I think he likes *me*.

Chapter 20

'It's just a few people getting together at a friend's house,' I tell Mum. What I don't tell her is that this friend is not my friend at all – I don't know her. Donna, Tara and Abby used to go to school with her, so technically she is *someone's* friend. Technically I'm not lying.

'Hmm. Which friend is this?' Mum's picked at the hole in my story.

'Harriet,' I say.

'There's no Harriet at Hillcrest.' Mum's even managed to drag her eyes away from her screen for long enough to look at me.

'She—'

'Have you got make-up on?' Mum interrupts.

'Not really,' I say. I'm wearing mascara and lipstick.

Mum shakes her head. 'Is this girl older than you?' She looks me up and down like I'm a contestant at a modelling show. I'm wearing black tights under jean shorts and a loose pink T-shirt that Donna lent me. She said this would make me look as if I hadn't made an effort, but would make me look nice too. And if the T-shirt slips down at one side and shows my bra strap — apparently that's a good thing. 'Do her parents know you're coming?'

'Of course!' I say. 'They'll be there.'

Mum's eyes fall on to my trumpet case. I'm so stupid! I should have left it in the hall.

Her eyes narrow suspiciously. 'Why are you taking that?'

'Erm . . .' There's no way to handle this except to tell the truth. 'My friends have a band and they wanted me to play with them for a bit. Just for tonight,' I add quickly. 'Just for this party.'

Mum raises an eyebrow. 'So now it's a party?'

Dad sticks his head around the door, a big grin on his face. 'Who said something about a party?'

'Nothing, Dad,' I say with a sigh.

'Your daughter has joined a band. She's

trying to sneak off to a strange girl's party to play with them.'

'Really?' he says.

He sounds impressed. I nod. 'But not *really* really.' I'm not exactly sneaking off; I told her where I was going. And I haven't even officially joined the band. 'It's just for tonight.'

Dad gives Mum a hopeful look. 'I don't mind taking her.'

'No,' Mum says. 'I don't think she should go.'

'Come on, Mum!' I plead. 'We break up for holidays next week.'

'And I'm off to the jazz club anyway,' Dad tries again. 'I could pick her up on the way back.'

Great. Dad's off to meet Miss Rotimi. OK, I don't know that for sure. But he's going to the club so there's a chance she'll be there.

Mum sends Dad a meaningful glare to say she doesn't want to talk about it in front of me. But also lets us both know we're in trouble.

'Look, forget it,' I say, turning and heading up to my bedroom. I don't want to be the cause of yet another argument. 'I'll just say I can't go.'

I hear them talking as soon as I'm out the door. They aren't shouting, so that's good, but I know I've triggered another *discussion*. Their discussions are always about me. Going to a party to play with Sucker Punch isn't worth my parents' marriage. It's hanging by a thread as it is.

I get into my room, and I'm tempted to throw my trumpet out of the window. But I don't. My trumpet is the only good thing in my life at the moment. Instead I flop on the bed and get out my phone.

Sorry guys. Can't come tonight. Parents are evil. Break a leg x x

I text this to Donna and Lenny, but of course Donna doesn't know I have Lenny's number so she thinks it's just for her.

☹ *I'll let you know all the goss tomorrow x x*

Lenny texts back too:

Nooooooo! Stage a prison break. We need you!

Lenny's message makes me smile . . . then makes me want to cry.

I open up my trumpet case and get it out. I shone it especially this afternoon. In fact, I think I spent more time shining my trumpet and oiling the valves than I did getting my look right. Donna would have been shocked. But then her instrument is her voice – she wouldn't have to do anything to make it prettier, except apply more lipstick.

I lift the trumpet to my lips and start to play. This time I'm not using music to block out my parents arguing, just to practise the tune I won't be performing.

There's a knock on the door.

'Come in,' I say.

Dad sticks his head round. 'I've been knocking for the past five minutes,' he says.

'Sorry,' I say. 'Couldn't hear you.' And I hold up my trumpet as an explanation.

'You sounded really good,' he says. 'You must be practising hard.'

I want to tell him the truth, that yes, even though it's only been a few days I've already improved from practising with Lenny. And, though I hate to admit it, those couple of times with Miss Rotimi in the orchestra helped too.

It's not just that I want to be in a band any more; I need it.

'Come on then,' he says.

'*Come on then*, what?' I say.

He motions to the door. 'Do you want a lift to this party or not?'

My face bursts into a grin. 'Really? Mum said I can go?!'

'Er . . .' Dad looks behind him, then whispers, 'Quick! Before she realizes what we're up to.'

I jump off the bed and put my trumpet back in its case. I try not to think about how Mum will flip her lid when she realizes I've gone to this party after telling me I couldn't. And I *really* try not to think about the fact that Mum and

Dad's row will be the biggest ever because Dad helped me.

But I want to go. I want to play with Sucker Punch and hang out with my friends. I want to see the look on Donna's face when I take the stage with her. And I want to see how happy Lenny is that I could make it after all.

'Thanks, Dad, you're the best,' I tell him as we creep downstairs.

'Let's hope your mother sees it that way,' he says.

Chapter 21

Our car pulls up outside the party house. I can tell it's the party house because of the steamed-up windows and the shadows of the people dancing. Even though it's a freezing night in the middle of December it must be hot in there; the front door is open and a couple of adults are watching over a few people spilling out into the front garden. I can't see anyone I know.

I text Lenny.

Come outside. There's a surprise waiting for you in the driveway . . .

'Don't be nervous, love,' my dad says, leaning past me to see the kids I'm looking at. 'You'll do great.'

I grimace at him. 'How do you know?'

'No performance is ever perfect. But that's

not what people like about live music. The thing is to relax and look comfortable when you're playing.'

'But I'm completely *un*comfortable!' I yelp.

'Then fake it,' he replies.

More lies. I take another deep breath.

'I'm very proud of you, you know,' he says.

'Thanks, Dad.'

'And don't worry – I'll square it with your mother.'

It will take a whole geometry set of squaring to fix this. She said I couldn't go and Dad took me anyway. I'm worried that my selfish need to come to this party might be the thing that breaks them. The dinner I'm going to cook tomorrow is going to have to be really, really great to make up for all this.

A body pushes out from among the people crowded by the front door. It's Lenny looking around for his surprise, and he looks so cute because he's confused.

I giggle. 'That's my friend,' I tell my dad, leaning over to give him a kiss on the cheek. 'Thanks for the lift.'

Dad's eyes are glued on Lenny. '*That's* your friend. That quiff?'

I laugh again. 'It's OK, Dad. He's just a friend.'

He shakes his head and mutters something I don't understand in his Nigerian patois. I make my escape before he locks the car doors.

'Be out here at ten o'clock,' he calls after me. 'Don't be late, or I'll come in and find you. Loudly!'

I turn back and wave at him.

Lenny's spotted me getting out of the car and he bounds forward. 'I thought you said you couldn't come,' he says, and gives me a hello hug.

'I had an accomplice,' I tell him, thumbing at Dad, who's still watching us.

'Nice one, Obi's dad,' Lenny says, nodding his head in approval.

I feel shy because all the people I don't know – the ones waiting by the door – are watching us. Lenny's so handsome he's hard to miss, and he's hugging me. So once again all eyes are sort of on me.

'What's the party like?' I ask.

'Good,' he says. 'You've come at a perfect time. We've just played our first of two sets. People were pretty OK with it and a few girls were dancing. But I think it was a good warm-up for the next one. Then everyone will start moving, I reckon.'

'Especially when you play *Solo No More*,' I say, which is my favourite of all Sucker Punch's songs.

'Especially when we beef it up a notch with your trumpet sounds.'

It's awesome to be at my first gig – if I can call playing at a birthday party that. But although I'm excited to have an audience at last, it makes it all much scarier.

Lenny takes my hand and leads me through the people and inside the house. I can't believe we're holding hands! I'm using all my concentration to try and not sweat too much. I don't want him to think I'm disgusting.

'Hello,' say the adults at the door, who I assume are Harriet's parents.

'I don't think we've met . . . ?' says the dad.

'My name's Obi,' I say. But the raised eyebrow shows he wants more.

'She's with the band,' says Lenny, and I smile because Lenny's taking this 'gig' stuff so seriously. If I try hard enough, I can imagine we're at a real gig and he's guiding me through the stage door.

Now everyone's *really* looking. Not only because I'm *with the band* but because Lenny's with me. I think they think I'm Lenny's girlfriend. It's nice to let them think that for a second.

'Obi! Is that you?!' I turn round to see Tara and Abby chatting to some girls I've never seen before.

They come over. I drop Lenny's hand but it's too late, they've seen. Abby grins at me but doesn't say anything.

'I didn't know you two were coming,' I say. 'How cool!'

'Yeah, we were friends with Harriet at Rimewood. Right, Abby?'

Abby nods, but she's still smiling down at my hand.

'Harriet asked Donna if Sucker Punch could

play here. Then when she found out that I'm Reece's girlfriend she invited me along too. And I invited Abby.'

Abby drags me away from Lenny to the room where everyone has put their coats. Tara comes too.

'What are you doing here?' says Abby, wiggling her eyebrows. 'Did Lenny bring you?' She wants the gossip. 'Does Donna know you're here?'

'No,' I say quickly, throwing my coat on to a pile. 'I thought I couldn't come, but – ' I hold up my trumpet case – 'I'm playing with Sucker Punch.'

'Oh cool!' Tara and Abby say at exactly the same time.

'Can we watch when she sees you?' Tara has a wicked twinkle in her eye.

'Erm, sure.' Donna's going to be jealous that I've arrived with Lenny. And my instinct says she has a right to be.

'Hurry up,' Lenny says, sticking his head around the door. 'Harriet doesn't want the music to stop for too long.'

I'm pleased he doesn't take my hand this time as he pushes a path through the people in the party. There's a room with a door open and they've got a movie playing, but there are only a few people in there. Almost everyone is in the living room where the music is. Someone's iPod is playing – some indie stuff I half recognize – I guess to fill in before Sucker Punch starts up again.

The door to the lounge is open and the room looks huge. It's full, but really there are probably only about twenty people here. The band are set up in one corner, with Reece on drums taking up most of the space at the back and then Donna's mic and amp at the front, with two large speakers at either side. Harriet's mum is pouring out cups of lemonade.

'Hey, guys,' Lenny calls out. 'Remember I said I had a surprise for you?'

Donna looks up hopefully. She smiles at Lenny, then sees me standing next to him.

Lenny holds out his arm as if introducing me for the first time.

'Erm . . . surprise,' I say.

Chapter 22

'Obi!' Donna cries. 'This *is* a surprise. Brilliant!' She steps forward and links her arm in mine. 'I'm really pleased you're here. They're a tough crowd.'

I chuckle. 'Come on, Donna. This is a birthday party, not a concert at the Brixton Academy!' But inside I feel nervous. My first gig, and it's a tough one.

'If we're going to make it we've got to act like every performance is the Brixton Academy,' she scolds.

She's not helping my nerves. What if I ruin it for them?

'We've warmed them up,' she continues. 'But I think they were expecting the Arctic Monkeys or something, and all they got was us.'

'They're lucky to have you, right, guys?' I say, doing my best to keep up morale.

Joel cringes. Reece shrugs. 'I guess,' he says.

'Of course they are,' says Tara. 'But maybe you should start the next set with some covers. Everyone loves a good cover.'

Sucker Punch does have some great songs, but unless you are one of the thirty-seven people subscribed to their YouTube channel, you wouldn't know any of them.

'It's a good idea, Tara,' says Lenny. 'What do you say, guys?'

Joel crosses his arms in front of his chest, which isn't easy because of his guitar. 'We're wasting our time writing songs if, when we play for real, all we do is churn out other people's stuff.'

'He has a point,' says Abby, who was always going to side with Joel.

Donna glares at her. 'How about this? We start the set with *Valerie*, to get the crowd going. Then we move on to our own stuff.' She sidles over to Joel. 'It's not as if we weren't going to play it anyway.'

He sighs. 'All right.'

'Great solution,' I say. 'Well done, Donna.'

Donna smiles at me. A smile that shows her teeth. She is happy that I'm here. Genuinely.

But then I start to move towards her – on to the stage area – and she frowns. 'Sorry, Obi,' she says, 'there really isn't room for you to listen from here. We're cramped enough as it is.'

'Erm . . .' I look at Lenny to help me out.

'Playing *Valerie* first is a particularly brilliant solution, Donna,' he says, 'because it's one of the ones Obi and I have been practising.'

'You and Obi have been practising?' Donna scrunches up her face. 'When?' Her voice wobbles a bit.

This is not how I wanted it to come out. I feel really bad for not telling her – especially as we're best friends now. I should have said something before. But I decided on secrets and lies.

'Obi's learned all our songs,' says Lenny. 'We've worked out when she should come in and it'll sound great.'

'But . . . but . . .' Donna's lost for words. Which doesn't happen often.

'Surprise,' I say again, feebly.

'But we haven't rehearsed,' says Joel.

'Obi knows what she's doing,' Lenny tells him. 'Just play as normal and she'll do the rest.'

I'll do the rest?! That's quite a lot of pressure.

'Are you sure you can do this?' asks Joel.

'Yes,' Lenny says for me.

'Er . . . no,' I say for myself. 'But I'll give it a go.'

'There's no harm in letting her try,' says Tara. 'Just for one song, at least.'

'Yeah!' says Donna, jumping on board. 'Come on, Obi, let's see what you can do.' She moves to the side and lets me on to the stage area.

I put my case down behind Reece's drum kit and get out my trumpet.

'You ready?' says Donna, smiling at me.

'As I'll ever be,' I say. I push the deceit out of my mind and start getting excited about performing with my best friend.

'Then let's go.'

She steps forward and turns on the mic. She signals to Lenny, who turns off the iPod. Everyone in the party swings round to look at us. I feel a rush of blood from my stomach to my ears, but weirdly, it feels kind of good. This is not like a trumpet exam where I'm all on my own; it's me with a group. We're sharing the glare. And that makes it OK.

'Hello, Harriet's house!' Donna yells.

No one says anything.

'I *said* . . . "Hel-lo Harriet's house!"' she tries again.

Brixton Academy, eat your heart out.

Tara and Abby shout, 'Hello!' at the top of their voices, because they're good sports. A couple of people mutter a hello, then laugh.

'Thanks to our two fans there,' says Donna, smiling at Tara and Abby, making a joke of it. 'We'll pay you after.'

If Donna's nervous, she's brilliant at disguising it. A true professional, just like Dad said.

'You guys were really great in our first set,' Donna says to the crowd. 'We thank you.' She's even made that lie seem convincing.

'You were so great we've decided to bring in a special treat for you . . . On trumpet: Obi Udogu!' She turns around to smile toothily at me. 'The newest member of Sucker Punch, and my best friend.'

Not hidden away behind her any more, I feel scared again.

'Wave to the nice people, Obi,' she says.

I hold up my hand.

'Now curtsy,' she adds.

Er . . .

'Joking,' Donna says. This gets a real and actual laugh from the crowd and I see how skilled Donna is. She was born to do this.

'Let's get on with it, shall we?' she says to us. Then to the crowd, 'I think you're going to like this one.'

Reece starts up with the drums and a few people catch on straight away to the song we're playing. A couple of people start dancing. Even Harriet's mum and dad are swaying in the background.

Donna sings, '♫ *Well sometimes I go out by myself and I look across the water* ♫'

She doesn't do it in an Amy Winehouse voice, like I've heard so many people trying to do; she does it in her own voice. I have to wait until the chorus before I kick in with my part.

Lenny looks at me as I'm just about to come in. I put the trumpet to my lips and let go. The notes come easily, without me having to really think. I'm starting to enjoy myself, and the crowd are too – just like Dad said they would. And what's weird is that I'm not having to fake it at all.

Playing with a band is where I'm supposed to be.

Then Harriet's mum comes into the room talking to a woman. It's Mum! And she looks furious. She's talking politely to Harriet's parents, but even from here I can see her eyes blazing with fury. She's crossed her arms and she's tapping her fingers.

I am in so much trouble now. Thank God she seems to be waiting until the end of the song before she drags me offstage. I'm tempted to stop playing and make a run for it, but it would draw too much attention to myself.

But when I dare to glance at Mum again, she

doesn't look angry any more. She's uncrossed her arms. Her fingers are tapping, but now they're tapping along to our beat. And what's more . . . she's smiling.

Chapter 23

The round of applause feels wonderful. I get it now – why half the kids in my school want to be famous. There is a whole party full of people I don't know and they're all gazing at me like I'm a celebrity. The smiling, the clapping, the whooping – I could live off this.

'Thank you, everyone, but we've already done much more that we said we would,' Donna calls. 'The encore was a total unexpected surprise.'

The encore was actually more rehearsed than the rest of it – Lenny told me. It needs more preparation as it's supposed to look like we've just come up with it.

Donna turns to the rest of the band and claps to thank us. We smile and wave and clap at her.

Mum's still standing at the back of the room pretending she's nothing to do with me. As she's white and I'm black, I don't think anyone will guess we're related. It's weird, but now she's here I sort of want to show her off. She's my mum. And although she's been a massive grump recently, I love her. I wave at her, nervous that her smiles are just a facade. But the best thing about mum is that she *doesn't* fake it — she honestly isn't angry any more.

She raises her hand to give a subtle wave back.

Abby follows my eye line and I can see from her face that she's trying to work out who this woman is.

Lenny comes over and whispers, 'Is that your mum?'

I smile proudly. 'Yup.'

He nods. Then gives her a thumbs-up.

'Stop flirting with the ladies,' says Joel. 'You'll get a reputation.' And we all have a little laugh.

'Thank you, everyone! You've been awesome!' Donna shouts. 'We've been Sucker Punch and I hope you've enjoyed listening to us tonight.'

Another loud cheer.

'I'm going to say hi to Mum,' I tell the others. I put my trumpet down and squeeze across to her.

'Obi!' she says.

I hesitate before hugging her. She must be mad at me for being here, but she wraps her arms around me and squeezes tight. Then she pushes me back and away from her.

I bite my lip, waiting for the telling-off, but she just says, 'Oops! Am I allowed to hug you here?'

I smile. 'Of course!'

'Good.' She pulls me back in again.

'You're not cross that I came when you said that I couldn't?' I ask nervously.

Mum frowns. 'Well, yes, I am . . . very. When I realized your dad had snuck you out of the house I was livid. When I called him, he admitted you were here and I came straight over to drag you out . . .'

But for some reason, she didn't drag me out. 'So I'm in a lot of trouble?'

Mum looks to the ceiling. 'You are,' she says. 'Or you should be. But I heard you play!'

Mum sighs. 'Obi, you are fabulous. I'm so proud of you.'

'You have to say that because you're my mum.'

Mum shakes her head. 'No, I mean it. You – the whole group – you're really good.'

A little light switches on in my heart. 'Thanks.'

'I'm still furious with you for running off, but . . .' Her eyes go all misty and I'm afraid that all her good, non-embarrassing behaviour is about to go out the window and she's going to cry. 'I didn't understand before, and I'm sorry,' she says. 'This is a really big deal to you, isn't it?'

I nod. 'The biggest.'

I'm so relieved I could cry. Could it be that the power of the music has worked on my mum and she finally gets it? Like me and Dad get it.

'Schoolwork is still the most important,' she says, her warning tone back again, 'and I'm going to make you clean the bathroom till it's spotless as a punishment for tonight. But I see now that this is important too. I was wrong, and I'm sorry.'

Cleaning the bathroom every week for the rest of my life would be worth it if it means Mum's finally coming round.

'I wish your father was here,' she says, sounding dreamy.

'Hmm.' I'm trying not to think about what Dad's doing right now.

'You have real talent, Obi.' She goes all thoughtful again. 'In fact, I'm going to go into school on Monday and speak to that Miss Rotimi.'

My head starts to spin. If Mum speaks to Miss Rotimi, Miss Rotimi might let slip that she knows Dad and their affair could all come out. I hate that Dad's keeping this big secret. But the thought of Mum discovering the truth is a million times worse.

'What? Why?'

'You wanted to join orchestra and I didn't listen. I'm going to see if there's a way you can do orchestra without it affecting classes.'

'But, Mum, I don't even want to—'

'Well, now *I* want you to,' she says. 'I know your father will help – he could pick you up. Didn't you say Miss Rotimi runs a youth orchestra too? Maybe you could join that as well — as long as it fits in with school.'

Oh God, Mum's planning for me to spend all this time with the woman who is taking Dad away from our family.

Mum spots Tara's mum and waves at her. 'I'm going to talk to Julie for a minute.' Mum kisses me on the head. 'Meet you outside. And congratulate the band for me. Especially Donna — she's a star.'

I feel a huge lump in my throat. Mum and Miss Rotimi in the same room is the worst idea I can think of, but I have no idea how to stop it.

I head back to the band to pack up. Abby is helping Joel, making soppy eyes at him and laughing at everything he says.

Lenny looks at them and rolls his eyes. 'Where are *my* groupies?' he jokes.

'I'm sure it won't take long,' I say.

I put my trumpet into its case, still thinking about my parents. The room is emptying — someone has stuck the iPod back on, but it's ten o'clock and that's what time the party finishes. Everyone is putting their coats on.

'Didn't you have a coat?' Lenny asks me.

I nod. 'I put it in that massive pile in that room at the front. I'm never going to find it, am I?'

'Never,' Lenny says, shaking his head sadly. 'Start arranging the memorial service – the coat is gone.'

I whack him on the arm. 'Thanks for your support.'

Lenny laughs. 'Come on, I'll help you look.'

He grabs my hand. I look back to check on Donna, but she's deep in conversation with Harriet and her parents so she doesn't notice us. Lenny leads me into the room at the front. There is a girl there rifling through the coats, clearly trying to find hers.

'You haven't seen a black North Face, have you?' she says to us.

Almost every coat in here is a black North Face. 'Is it long or—'

'Here it is!' she cries, picking up her coat and hurrying from the room. 'Great party,' she says. 'You guys were awesome.'

I smile. Despite the mess with my mum and

Miss Rotimi, it's great to be told we sounded good. The door slams shut. Me and Lenny are alone with all the coats. He still has hold of my hand.

'My coat is a dark blue puffer thing,' I tell him, and go to pull my hand away.

But he pulls me back. I fall into him a little. 'Whoa! What are you up to?'

He laughs. 'I just . . . Just come here, will you?'

He leans his head forward. He has to lean down a long way because of his six-foot-two-ness. He's going to kiss me! My heart is beating so hard that it's hard to breathe. Do I want to kiss him?

I'm about to tell him no, but his lips are on mine.

Chapter 24

It's just a kiss on the lips at first. But it's a slow one. Then his lips open and his tongue comes out. Mine does too. I always thought touching tongues would be gross, but this is really nice. I don't know if it's the feeling of his lips and tongue moving against mine or because I'm tingling all over.

Lenny Fulton, the cutest boy in our year, is kissing me. He likes me. Little, skinny, frizzy-haired, stupid old me. I can't understand why he does, but I know the girls at school will go crazy when I tell them. When Reece and Tara first kissed it was all we talked about for weeks.

But of course, I can't tell the other girls. Not even Tara and Abby. If it got back to Donna she would die. And she's my best friend.

I step backwards, away from Lenny and his lovely kiss.

I smile up at him. 'That was . . .' I don't know how to finish the sentence.

'*That was . . . ?*'

I laugh, embarrassed. 'I have to go.'

'Obi,' he says, 'you really mean a lot to me.'

'I . . .' What do I say to that? 'Mum's waiting outside.'

He winces. 'Umm . . . OK.'

I quickly open the door so he doesn't try to kiss me again. I can't deny that I enjoyed that kiss, but I can't betray . . .

Donna.

She's standing right in the hallway. '*There you are!*' she says. 'Wasn't that amazing? The gig went really well, and your trumpet sounded gr—'

Lenny appears behind my shoulder and she stops talking. Her face falls.

'Oh, hi,' she says. 'What were you . . . ?'

She knows exactly what we were doing. My lips are still buzzy with the kiss and I wish I hadn't put on lipstick because I bet it's all over my face. I don't dare check Lenny's face, just in case he's covered in it too.

'I was just getting my coat,' I tell her, hoping she doesn't notice how flushed I must be.

Donna's lower lip has changed shape, like she's having to hold it in the right place. 'You're not going now too, are you?' she asks Lenny. 'I thought we were giving you a lift.'

Lenny nods far too quickly. 'I am . . . if that's still OK.' His voice is squeaky. Donna must know something's up.

'Well, anyway,' she says to me. 'That was great. Give me a call in the morning and we'll talk through the whole night.'

There's a lump of guilt in my throat so big I can't speak. I run out of the house and into the front garden where everyone is standing around, waiting for their parents to pick them up.

Only now that I'm outside and it's freezing do I realize: I forgot to get my coat! I'm such an idiot. But it's not really surprising after an awesome performance, then Mum saying she wants to speak to Miss Rotimi, then Lenny kissing me, then almost being busted by Donna. I'm losing my mind.

I run back into the room where the coats

are. But I stop when I hear Lenny. 'You really are a special girl, you know that?'

Who's he talking to? I peer round the side of the door. I see Lenny and his face is buried into long brown perfect hair. He's hugging her tightly, and then he gives her a kiss on top of her head.

'You really mean a lot to me,' he says.

I can't believe it; it's exactly what he said to me just two seconds ago! Why can't anyone tell the truth any more? Everyone is a liar.

Donna looks up at him. They lock eyes. 'You mean a lot to me too,' she says.

I can't watch them kiss. I turn and leg it, not caring about the coat.

I've been lying to Donna about Lenny. And now I find out Lenny is lying to us both.

Chapter 25

I cut the lasagne into six big pieces – one each, and one left over.

'Who's that one for?' Dad asks.

'Whoever gets there first,' I tell him.

'It's on!' says Jumoke, looking round the table, fork raised as if eating was a challenge.

I shake my head. 'This is supposed to be a civilized dinner,' I tell him. 'Not feeding time at the pigpen.'

Mum laughs. She rests back in her chair, glass of wine in hand. 'Don't take it personally, Obi,' she says to me. 'All men are the same. I once asked your father if he'd like me to put his food in the blender so he could use a straw!'

We all start laughing.

'He actually considered it!' she adds.

'It's not such a bad idea,' says Dad.

Mum takes another sip of her wine and throws out her hand. 'You see,' she says, but I'm pretty sure she's just teasing him.

As I heap a portion of lasagne on to each plate and pass them across, I look around the table. Everyone is smiling. Mum's computer has been banned from the room. Bem laid the table and even lit a candle in the middle. Jumoke was in charge of garlic bread and salad, while I did the lasagne.

'Why haven't they just invented a pill that gives you all the food you need for the day?' I ask.

Mum leans forward and lays a hand on my arm. 'Because this is really lovely,' she says seriously. 'I really appreciate my children going to all this effort.'

Dad smiles at us too. 'It is. Thank you. What's the occasion?'

'No occasion,' I say. 'I just thought it would be nice for us all to spend time together.'

Mum nods. 'You're right,' she says. 'I'm sorry I've been so busy recently.'

I panic. I don't want it to kick off again. 'I

didn't mean it like that, Mum. I wasn't having a go.'

She raises her hands in surrender. 'I know you weren't,' she says. 'I just want you all to know that I appreciate you being patient with me while work is so full on. I promise, after Christmas, the project will be in hand – fingers crossed – and things will be different.'

Christmas is just over a week away. Somehow I doubt it'll all be tied up by then.

Right on cue, her mobile rings.

I hold my breath.

She grabs the phone from where it's lying just in front of her. She looks at the display, is about to hit the screen when she stops. She shakes her head. 'It can go to voicemail. Tonight's my night off.' But her eye is still on the screen. That wasn't easy for her.

Dad sits back down and raises his glass. 'Cheers to that!'

We all lift our glasses and say, 'Cheers.' Then Bem starts scarfing down his food. All the time he keeps watch on the extra slice.

We laugh again and I feel really proud of

myself. This was all Lenny's idea, but I pulled it off. I can't fix the mess that's going on with me and Donna and Lenny — all the secrets and the two-timing. What worries me is that Donna hasn't been in touch. I've called, but she's not answering. Lenny's called me, and I'm not answering. But his suggestion to make dinner might have just fixed my family. Mum and Dad seem to be getting on tonight. Hopefully, if all goes well, Dad won't go off with Miss Rotimi.

'So,' Mum says, in between bites, 'what's been going on with all of you? How's school?'

'Meh,' says Bem.

'Meh too,' says Jumoke.

'Meh three,' I add.

'Well, that was a wonderfully informative conversation, thank you,' says Dad.

'Here's me worrying that I've missed out so much,' Mum says. She and Dad exchange looks, laughing at us. It's nice to see them bond, even at our expense.

'How are you feeling about your GCSE mocks in January?' she says to Jumoke.

Jumoke winces. 'Don't want to talk about it.

All the teachers are getting really stressed with us. It's not helping! I need a calm and clear mind.'

'Don't worry, your mind is clear,' I tell him. 'Too clear. It's empty!'

'Thanks a lot, super-stink,' he says.

'Obi's only saying that because she's teacher's pet,' says Bem.

I narrow my eyes at him. 'Whose pet am I supposed to be?'

'That new music teacher,' Jumoke chips in, siding with Bem. 'Whassa name? Miss Rotimi.'

I hold my breath. Dad stops chewing his food. He looks at me and we catch eyes so he has to look down at his plate.

'She's not a real teacher,' I growl. 'And I'm not her pet.' And I feel disgusted with myself for ever being proud that she singled me out.

'You totally are,' says Bem.

'She is,' Jumoke says to Mum.

'Are you?' Mum asks me, light-heartedly. 'Having heard you last night, I wouldn't be surprised.'

'I'm not,' I say, pushing my salad around with my fork. 'In fact, I hate her.'

232

Dad, who has stayed suspiciously out of the conversation up till now, and not mentioned the fact that he meets up with her at the club all the time, suddenly snaps his head up. '*Hate* is a very strong word, Obi.'

'Well, I do.'

As if Dad wants me to blurt out why.

'I think there's a story here,' says Mum, a little tipsy now with the wine. 'Come on, spill.'

'It's nothing!' I say.

'So,' says Bem, 'we were outside playing football while some sad little orchestra thing was going on in the school. This woman comes out – this Miss Rotimi – calls Obi over and asks her if she would play trumpet in the orchestra.'

'Then I heard,' says Jumoke, loving that he gets to pile in on the teasing, 'that at the singing auditions for the Christmas concert, she made Obi audition.'

'Yeah,' I say, 'she basically forced me to sing. That's one of the reasons why I hate her.'

'How did she even know you play the trumpet?' asks Mum.

I look at Dad to explain, but he is staring at his salad like it's a map to hidden treasure.

'I don't know,' I say.

'*Hmm.*' Mum looks very thoughtful. 'This just confirms my plan: I'll find a moment to get away from work and have a word with her.'

'I don't think it's a good idea,' Dad pipes up.

'But, Tumo,' Mum says, 'if Obi's teacher thinks she's special—'

Dad shakes his head rapidly. 'We've been through this already. Obi's schoolwork will suffer. It'll be bad for her education. Like you said.'

Dad's arguing against everything he argued for last time, and it's so obvious why. Obvious to me.

'It's not a problem,' I say quickly, 'because I don't want to be in the orchestra anyway. I already told her no.'

But this isn't about me apparently. Mum and Dad are looking for an excuse to fight and we've just given them one.

'I know what I said,' Mum growls at Dad, 'but maybe I was wrong.' She narrows her eyes. 'Are you just saying this to spite me?'

'No,' Dad spits back. 'I'd like Obi to be in a band. But this is something more than that. A band she can do in her free time. If it's a school orchestra they can pull her out of lessons. She'll miss classes.'

'What's up with you?' Mum scowls at him. 'Last time we spoke about this you were the one who wanted her to join orchestra. What's changed?'

I know what's changed: he doesn't want her finding out about his affair.

'Stop arguing, will you?' As much as I hate Dad right now, I don't want Mum finding out either. 'I don't want to be in orchestra. Orchestra is lame!'

The room goes silent. Bem and Jumoke look guilty for bringing it up. But it's not their fault — it's Dad's fault. He's the one having an affair.

'Look what you've done. Because of all your fuss,' Mum hisses at Dad, 'she won't even consider it now. You weren't thinking of her education when you snuck her out of the house last night.'

Dad throws down his knife and fork. 'I knew you were still narked about that!'

My parents are fighting again, and it's about me. Again. I've had enough. I stand up. They all look at me. 'I'm not feeling well.' I walk out of the dining room.

'Obi!' says Mum. 'Please come back. We're sorry. Your father and I can talk about this later.'

But I ignore her.

Behind me I can hear Dad push his chair back. 'I have to make a call,' he says.

I bet he's calling Miss Rotimi.

'I thought we said no phones?' Jumoke mutters.

But Dad has already gone past them and me and upstairs into the bedroom, where he slams the door.

'It seems it's one rule for your father and another for everyone else,' says Mum.

I hate to admit it, but she's right. Dad is cheating on Mum and he doesn't want anyone to find out – so much so that he's willing to go back on everything he believes about music.

I know hate is a strong word, but I do hate Miss Rotimi. And what's worse, I'm starting to hate my dad too.

Chapter 26

'*Psst!* Oi! *Pssst!*'

Lenny's calling me. Instantly I blush and it must be so obvious.

'What?' I growl.

It's Monday break and this is the moment I was dreading: bumping into him.

'Hi there, groupie,' he says to me.

'I'm not your groupie,' I say, my voice still low.

'I know,' he says, shaking his head, his mouth drooping at the sides, pretending to be sad, 'but I think I might be *your* groupie.'

'Shut up.' He's flirting with me, but I saw him cuddling up with Donna.

'You kissed me, then ran off and left me!' he says. 'If that's not the kind of thing a musician does to an adoring fan, I don't know what is.'

I shove him all the way to the wall, my cheeks burning.

'Shh!' I say, and look around to see if anyone heard. Luckily none of the girls are around. It's just boys, and although a few of them have tuned in now that tiny little me has massive six-foot-two Lenny up against a wall, they didn't hear what he just said.

'Shh,' I say again, but this time with my voice lowered.

'Are you ashamed about kissing me?' He's smiling, teasing me, and despite how angry I am it's hard not to smile back. I push him into an empty classroom and close the door. He takes a step towards me, just like he did in the coat room at the party. I hold up my hand.

'First of all,' I say, 'you kissed *me*.'

'That's not how I remember it,' he says, grinning harder.

'Then you should get your brain checked,' I tell him. 'And second of all, you can't tell anyone.'

Lenny's face falls. 'Are you embarrassed to be my girlfriend?'

'I don't want to go out with you.' I pull a face like the thought disgusts me.

He looks away, good mood suddenly gone.

I can't believe this is real. Lenny says he wants me to be his girlfriend. Something twists inside me and all I can see is Donna's face. Then Lenny and Donna together in the coat room as they're about to kiss. Then I take in Lenny's face right now: he looks so hurt – his clenched jaw and slight frown. What a fake! He's just upset that I'm turning him down.

'Just leave me alone, will you?' I say.

'What's up?' he asks. 'Did something happen with your dad and Miss Rot—'

'Look!' I say, 'I don't want to talk about this. Especially not with you.'

'What have *I* done?'

I shake my head. Denying it makes it so much worse. 'Just go and talk to your girlfriend, will you? The girl who *really means a lot to you*.'

Lenny stares into my eyes. 'You know that's you.'

I can't believe he's such a liar.

'I heard you. At the party. I forgot my coat,

and when I went back to get it you had your arms wrapped around Donna and were telling her how special she is.'

Lenny takes a deep breath and slumps against the wall. 'I was . . .' He runs his fingers over his quiff. 'I was comforting her.'

'You were comforting Donna after her great performance?'

'No . . .' He looks like he's just stubbed his toe. 'There is a reason. There's something going on. And . . .'

'And?'

'And I can't say what.'

I sigh. 'That's convenient.'

'I would tell you, but then I'd have to kill you,' he tries with a cheeky smile.

He's using our thing to get back in my good books. I really, really want to believe he has an explanation for this. But I saw them.

'Whatever,' I say. I walk back towards the door.

Lenny grabs me by the arm. 'It's *you* I like.'

'Leave me alone.'

'Why don't you like me?'

God, it's so different for the beautiful people than it is for us mere mortals. Here's me, wondering why on earth he would like me. And there's him, wondering why I wouldn't like him back.

'That sounded pretty big-headed, didn't it?' he says. 'But what I meant was, we get on really well and we like each other. Why don't you want to be my girlfriend?'

'Because of Donna,' I tell him. 'She's my best friend. It's time I started acting like it.'

'But . . .'

'And that's also why I don't think I should be in Sucker Punch any more.' Saying the words out loud makes my heart hurt. I love music. I love playing in a band. But I have to give it up.

'No,' Lenny says.

'Yes.'

'Think about it before you decide,' he says desperately. 'I'll stay away from you . . . if you tell me to. But I know how much this music thing means to you. I think you want it more than the rest of us – not for the fame and money, but because you love to perform.'

I'd play even if no one was listening. For an empty stadium. I'd do it for free.

'I love my friends more,' I tell him.

He shakes his head. 'Don't let anything stand in the way of your dreams. Not Donna. Not even me.'

He's saying everything right. But even if I dare to believe he has an explanation for what happened at the party, I can't be with him. 'I can't hurt her,' I say.

'Then I'll tell her!' he says. 'I'll tell her that I don't like her in that way. And that I like you.'

Lenny clearly doesn't know anything about girls if he thinks she'd still be my friend after that. 'Don't say a word!'

There's a knock on the glass pane of the door.

I spin round to see Donna walking in.

'What are you two doing hiding in here?' she says. Her smile is fixed and fake. Lenny and I were talking about starting a relationship. It's her worst fear come true.

'We are . . .' I say, but I've no idea how to finish. Then I notice she's not in school uniform.

She's wearing jeans and an oversized jumper. 'Are you OK?' I ask. 'You weren't in registration this morning. You didn't message me back yesterday.'

She shakes her head. 'Umm. Not really.'

'Are you sick?' I ask her.

She takes a deep breath. 'My dad moved out.' She flips her hair.

What?!

'Yeah. My parents are getting a divorce,' she says. But in this weird, not worried way, like she's talking about a character in a soap or something.

It takes a second for her words to sink in. Then I rush forward and hug her. I want to comfort my poor friend. But right now I feel dirty with the guilt.

'Oh my God!'

Donna pulls away from me and shrugs. 'I'm fine. I kind of guessed it was coming. My dad's never at home. It was always on the cards.'

She said this about her dad before: how he's never around, all the tense silences. But I wasn't listening close enough to get it. Have I been a bad friend to her just like I thought she was a bad friend to me?

'But the good thing is, they've let me off school!' Her eyes are wide with excitement. 'I know we break up on Wednesday, but still.'

There's no way she could be OK with this.

Lenny stammers a little. 'I-I'll leave you girls to it.' He keeps his eyes away from mine as he rushes out the room. I feel so bad – I've broken the Girl Code. I want to tell Donna, but after her revelation my timing couldn't be worse.

'What's his problem?' Donna asks me.

I shrug. 'Monday morning?'

Donna's staring at the door Lenny's just walked through.

'I was thanking him for getting me to come along on Saturday night,' I say hurriedly. 'That's what we were talking about. But tell me about your parents. What's—'

'Forget about it,' she says. 'It's boring. I have to tell you something much more interesting.'

I don't get her. My parents might be on the brink of divorce and it's killing me. But her parents have actually said the words – her dad has actually moved out – and she seems completely cool with it.

'The party was excellent,' she says, 'but what happened *after* was even better.'

'What happened after?' I say. I can't make her talk about her parents, so I play along.

'Me and Lenny.'

My heart speeds up. 'What about you and Lenny?'

She looks round to see if anyone's eaves-dropping. Though actually I think she *wants* people to hear. 'We kissed!'

I feel like I'm falling. So Lenny *did* kiss her. He lied to me about having an explanation. My instincts about him were wrong and I feel like I never knew him at all. Which is even worse.

But something in the back of my head says, *Is this another one of Donna's lies?*

'Really? Wow!' My voice comes out all strange-sounding. I cough to fix it. 'What happened?'

'First he put his arms round me in that room where all the coats were. Just after you left, he pulled me back in there and tried to kiss me.'

Just like he did with me. This is the way he gets girls. Me, Donna, who knows who else?

'We were about to kiss but people kept walking in so we couldn't,' she says.

I'm relieved, but only a little, because there's more to come.

'Then my mum arrived to pick us up,' she continues. Listening to this is worse than my brother's drum and bass. 'She took us back to my place and Lenny asked if he could come in. Because he lives round the corner, Mum said it would be OK.'

'What happened then?' I know I have the same fixed smile that Donna wears when she sees me and Lenny together.

'While I was making us one of my amazing hot chocolates, he said he wanted to help. He was getting really close to me, brushing past me to get stuff from the cupboard and the fridge. Coming up behind me to *"check my method"*. I could feel his breath in my ear.' She closes her eyes tight, remembering it. 'When I turned around he was right there. He leaned in . . .'

Now I close my eyes. I don't think I can hear this.

'And we kissed!'

I swallow hard. 'That's . . .'

'Isn't it amazing?!'

'Yeah. Great,' I say. 'I'm so happy for you.'

Lenny is a dog. A liar.

'We were properly snogging, but then my mum came in,' she finishes with a sigh. 'She ruined everything.'

'Oh! Total nightmare!' I overdo it but she doesn't seem to notice, too caught up in how happy she is.

'I know,' she says. 'Parents, eh? Who'd have them?'

Between my parents and my friends, I could live without them both.

Hang on a minute . . . something about this revelation isn't quite right. 'Why didn't you tell me yesterday?' It's not like Donna not to tell me something like this the moment it happens. Especially not a *Lenny* something like this.

'I would have called, but then my parents

dropped the D-bomb.' She sighs as if her parents' split is just a minor frustration.

Donna lowers her voice. 'Besides, Lenny told me not to tell anyone. Sneak around to make it more fun.' She looks outside the door. 'But then I figured, you're not just anyone. Best friends tell each other everything, don't they?' She squeezes my arm so tight it hurts.

'Of course,' I say. Some best friend I am – I haven't told her a thing. And it means Lenny's been able to lie to us both.

Lenny said he liked me. He kissed me. But when I walked away, he was straight on to Donna.

'I'm going to be Lenny's girlfriend,' Donna says. 'I can feel it.'

This stings like a splinter. I know what this feeling is – jealousy. I was right when I said, *What you don't know doesn't hurt you.* But now I *do* know. And it hurts.

Chapter 27

Donna takes my arm and leads me outside. 'Poor you, having to stick around for classes,' she says. 'Dad's given me a load of money and I'm going shopping. Hit up the pre-Christmas sales. Shame you can't come too.'

She's still acting like the divorce is a good thing. I'm barely listening to her. My head is filled with Lenny's lies. The idea that he kissed me and then kissed her, and the fact I can't say anything about it.

'I'm going to buy Lenny a present,' she continues. 'What do you . . . ? Hey – isn't that your mum?'

My head snaps up. She's right. Mum is sitting reading a newspaper outside Mr Macadam's office.

Oh God. Mum's here to see Dad's mistress.

'Hello, Mrs Udogu!' Donna calls, waving like a maniac.

Mum looks up. 'Hello, girls,' she says, folding the paper and tucking it in her bag. 'I found I had a free moment so thought I'd head down to speak to Miss Rotimi.'

Donna twirls her hair around her finger. 'About what?'

Mum's going to tell Donna about orchestra. The first of many secrets I've been keeping. Luckily we're all distracted by a familiar noise – the Boys' School Girls. There are only ten girls in the whole school, but we make a different kind of noise to the boys so we're easily identified.

'That must be your friends,' says Mum with a grin.

'You hear it too?' I ask. 'I thought the calls of the lesser-spotted schoolgirls could only be heard by other lesser-spotted schoolgirls.'

Mum laughs. 'I was one once,' she says. 'And they haven't evolved much since then.'

And true to their habits, the girls come round the corner in a herd. Tara's holding hands with Reece. Lenny's hovering at the back, still looking miserable.

Tara sees us outside the office and she

bites her lip. 'Hello, Mrs Udogu.' She looks embarrassed — I'm guessing because she has no idea why Mum's here and she doesn't want to ask.

'Is this your mum, Obi?' Candy says. 'Hello, Mrs Udogu.'

Because of our skin colours, it takes a minute for the family resemblance to sink in. If you picture my mum with dark skin and dark hair you can see it — but you have to look hard.

'Don't worry,' I say to them. 'I'm not in trouble or anything.' I *am* in trouble . . . but not that kind.

Mum laughs. 'Not that I know of anyway,' she says. 'I've come to speak to Miss Rotimi. Obi, will you take me to her, please?'

I avoid looking at Lenny. He's the only one who knows how bad this could be.

'We'll come along too,' Indiana says.

'That's very kind.' Mum gets up and starts following them.

I hang my head all the way, trying to think of a way to get her to change her mind and go home.

We get near the music rooms and I hear something else that makes my stomach drop. The sound of a woman giggling. Her door has a window in it and Miss Rotimi has her eyes closed as she laughs. She's bending forward, placing her hand on a man's arm. He has his back to us, but I know who it is, just from his bald patch.

'Dad!' I say quickly, hoping Mum doesn't catch them touching.

Miss Rotimi pulls her hand back quickly. Dad jolts back too and stands up. I didn't know he was here. And from the flustered look on Mum's face, she had no idea either. Miss Rotimi on the other hand – she's smiling away. For some reason she's loving this.

The girls bump into my back, all trying to see what I'm staring at. 'Ob—' Dad's saying, but he stops when he sees the scene in front of him.

Mum's mouth is open. Her cheeks have gone pink.

This is awful.

'Dad,' I say again, trying to sound normal, 'what are you doing here?'

He looks at Mum and laughs nervously. 'I didn't know you were coming in today, Shannon.' Which might be an answer to my question, but it isn't a good one.

'I told you,' says Mum. 'I said I was going to speak to Miss Rotimi about getting Obi back into orchestra.'

Dad laughs again. 'How funny! That's what *I'm* doing here!' He's speaking too loudly.

Mum smiles at the pair of them, but it's not a real smile. This is the moment she realizes her husband is having an affair.

My friends are looking between all the adults. They don't know what's going on but they can sense it's not good.

I run forward to get in the middle of Mum and Dad and force a laugh. 'Ha ha! You've *both* come in to do the same thing!' I look at Miss Rotimi and then at Mum. 'I don't know if that makes you super-organized, or super-*dis*organized.'

I'm using my rubbish jokes to try to lighten the mood and help Dad cover his tracks. He's so in the wrong here, but I'll help him if it means my parents won't break up.

Mum's still staring hard at him. 'I thought you were at work today, Tumo?'

'Early lunch.'

'Ahh,' says Mum, nodding, but she doesn't look convinced.

'Anyway,' I say, 'about orchestra,' I look at Miss Rotimi. It takes all my strength not to piledrive her like I've seen the wrestlers do on Bem's favourite show.

'What about orchestra?' says Donna, frowning at me.

Hannah whispers in my ear. 'Orchestra is so lame.'

'You stopped coming to rehearsals, Obi,' says Miss Rotimi.

I feel the stares of all the girls on me.

'Since when were you going to rehearsals?' asks Donna.

I don't answer.

'You've already been going to rehearsals?' asks Mum.

Again I don't reply. Instead I say to Miss Rotimi, 'I've missed too much, haven't I? It's too late for me to join orchestra now. There'd be too much to catch up on. School's over on Wednesday and the concert is on Saturday. There's no way. It's pointless.'

Abby giggles nervously at my babbling. So do the others. They think I'm trying to get out of orchestra because it's 'lame', when really I think it's anything but. The reason I want out of orchestra is so much bigger. I'm trying to keep my family together.

'You're probably right about that,' Miss Rotimi says. Then she looks at my dad. 'But we have some good news.' She bats her eyelashes at him.

Since when did *they* become *we*? It feels like they're just about to tell us they've started dating. Mum looks even more uncomfortable, her teeth clenched.

'Do we?' says Dad.

He's not doing very well at this. He's supposed to be here to talk about orchestra, but it's clear he doesn't have a clue what she's on about.

'As well as being an accomplished trumpeter,' Miss Rotimi says, 'you're a very good singer.'

I close my eyes. This just gets worse and worse.

'It's just the one song, so it'll be easy to get up to speed,' she says. 'And she'll be singing with this handsome chap over here.' She points at Lenny. 'Obi, Lenny, I'd love it if you'd do the duet at the concert on Saturday.'

Mum raises both eyebrows. 'Singing too?' she says. 'I had no idea how talented you are, Obi.'

I certainly seem to have a talent for getting into messes.

'We'll put in extra practices all this week,' Miss Rotimi says. 'After school, and longer sessions on Thursday and Friday once school breaks up. That way you won't miss class.'

'I'd be happy to help too,' says Dad. 'I could give you a lift.'

Lenny's grinning like he's just won the lottery.

But when I turn to Donna, her face is the exact opposite. Her mouth has fallen open and she's gone pale.

I've taken the singing part she wanted. And I'll be singing with Lenny – the boy Donna wants. And worse still, Dad will be able to see

Miss Rotimi whenever he likes because they can disguise it as helping me.

This is a nightmare.

The girls stare at Donna. She looks like a statue. It's so silent and awkward.

'Oh my god,' says Candy nervously. 'Umm . . . congratulations, Obi!'

'Yeah, big congrats!' Abby joins in.

Then they all do, almost bowling me over with a group hug.

I've had so much information in the last twenty minutes that my head is spinning and I can't take it any more. It takes me a while to work out what they're congratulating me for – for my dad running off with my teacher? Or for breaking my best friend's heart?

Chapter 28

Breathing is difficult in the middle of this hug of girls.

'We all assumed Donna would get it,' says Indiana. 'But it's cool that you've got a turn at singing. Right, Donna?'

I push them all away to look for Donna. I know her better than the rest of them and know that this double blow won't be good for her. I look past the girls – and there's just a half-empty corridor with posters on the wall to advertise the Christmas concert. Donna must have run off. She must be devastated, and it's all my fault. Lenny's lurking by the wall, frowning and pale – he knows how much we've hurt Donna, and with what she's going through at home, it's the last thing she needs.

He and I exchange a look. I didn't want to steal him away from Donna, but weirdly, me and him are now in this together. We're a couple in this world of guilt.

'And, Lenny,' says Indiana, noticing him there, 'congratulations to you too.'

'Umm, thanks,' he says. He's looking past her, further down the corridor. I follow his eye line and spot Donna walking away.

I leave them all and go after her.

'Donna!' I yell.

She doesn't stop so I have to run.

When I catch up, the sight of her makes my heart burst. Her mouth is set into a grim line and she looks like she's the ghost in a horror movie. Nothing worse could happen to her. I wish I could jump into the floor and put the lino back over me. I don't deserve the solo. I don't deserve to have a best friend.

'I've no idea why Miss Rotimi gave me the part,' I tell Donna. Except I do – she gave it to me because she's in love with my dad and he probably asked her to. 'But everyone in the school knows it should have been yours.'

'I think *I* know why,' says Sonia.

I turn round. All the girls are there and

Sonia's at the front of them, smiling evilly, her eyes twinkling. This is so not the time for Sonia's stirring. If she knew Donna's parents were divorcing then she wouldn't be doing this. I wish I could tell her, but once again, this is Donna's secret. All I can do is shoot Sonia a look to tell her to shut up.

She ignores it. Even smirks at me to let me know she isn't going to shut up. Not at all.

'I'm nowhere near as good as Donna,' I say, glaring at Sonia, willing her to be nice.

'You're right,' says Sonia. 'You aren't.'

I relax a little.

'But Lenny is the best male singer. And he doesn't have the chemistry with Donna.'

The girls are silent. They can't believe Sonia's being so mean about Donna in front of everyone.

'He has chemistry with you,' Sonia continues.

'It's not true,' I say to Donna.

But it *is* true. Even though I've been surrounded with lies recently — most of them my own — I know the truth when I hear it.

'So if Miss Rotimi wants the best performance,' Sonia continues, 'she has to pick the best couple. Lenny and Obi are made for each other.'

Now I'm furious. 'Shut up, Sonia!' Even if she doesn't know what Donna's going through at home, she's still publicly humiliating her.

'Shut up, Sonia,' Lenny repeats.

Donna's eyes are blazing.

'I think she only picked me because she's . . .' I hesitate over the word, '*friends* with my dad.' There's so much more to it than that. If I could explain it all, then maybe Donna would understand.

She won't look at me.

She doesn't say anything.

'Don't be upset, Donna,' I tell her.

'I'm not upset!' she yells. 'But I'm annoyed . . . with myself . . . for being best friends with such a cow!'

The girls gasp. Tara says, 'Hey!' sticking up for me. 'It's not cool to call Obi names.' But if she knew how completely and utterly I've broken the Girl Code, I think she'd join in.

'It makes me never want to sing again,' she says.

I can't help but laugh. 'Now you're being ridiculous,' I tell her. 'Your voice——'

She cuts me off. 'It's over,' she says.

'What's over?' I ask, really hoping she's not going to say our friendship, even though I can't see a way to save it now.

'Sucker Punch,' she says.

I gasp. 'What do you mean?'

'Donna——' Lenny starts.

Donna cuts him off. 'I'm done with the group. You can be the vocalist, Obi. I'm not doing it any more. Not with you.'

I shake my head rapidly. 'No!' I can't be responsible for breaking Sucker Punch like I've broken up my parents' marriage. '*I'll* leave. You've always been the lead woman. I'm nothing compared to you. Everyone knows it.'

'Not everyone apparently,' Donna says, jutting her chin into the air. 'You take Sucker Punch. You've taken everything else off me already.'

She pushes past me and stalks off.

'Please don't give up Sucker Punch,' I call after her, begging. 'Don't ruin our friendship.' I realize how much I enjoy spending time with her. She's not someone I ever thought I would bond with, but that makes it all the more real. I like her, and I like our differences. She seemed to like me too.

'I didn't ruin our friendship,' she says. '*You* did.'

She's right. I was the one who was keeping secrets and sneaking around behind her back. She might play a mean prank once in a while, but what I did was so much worse.

She's stormed off down the hall and I set off after her. The girls follow too, but I give them a look that tells them to back off.

Further down the corridor I can still hear footsteps behind me. Lenny's there, so I round on him.

'What are you doing?'

'If Donna's upset about Sucker Punch—' Lenny says.

'You think this is about Sucker Punch?! God, you really are stupid.'

It's all his fault. If he hadn't played us both and kissed us both, telling each of us what we wanted to hear . . .

'Just stay away, will you?' I say.

He stops running. 'OK,' he says. 'But call me if she needs me to explain. Call me and I'll—'

'Don't you get it?!' I explode. 'I said, *stay away.*'

Lenny flinches like I've punched him in the stomach. I feel as hurt as he looks. I can't fancy Lenny – not after he's betrayed both me and my best friend. If she even is my best friend any more.

'You've ruined my friendship with Donna,' I say to him. 'And I've never had a best friend before.'

'How did I—' he starts.

'You strung us along. Maybe you liked the attention. And for what? So you could mess around without the other finding out.'

'I'm not messing around with you,' he says. His eyes fill with tears and my heart twists like a sponge being wrung dry. I've never seen a boy cry before, except on a football pitch. I never thought a boy would cry over me. 'I really like you,' he says, and his voice cracks a little.

'Well, I don't like you,' I tell him.

His mouth curls in pain and it kills me. Hurting him is hurting me, but I have to make sure he knows I mean it.

'Not even as a friend.'

'Obi, I'm sor—'

I shake my head. 'Stay away from me forever.'

If I have to cut him out of my life to save my friendship with Donna, then that's what I'm going to do. It's the Girl Code. If only I had obeyed the Girl Code from the start, I wouldn't be in this mess. I wouldn't be losing my best friend.

Chapter 29

Now I know karma exists.

'I want you to look deep into each other's eyes,' says Miss Rotimi.

Practice with Lenny and Miss Rotimi is my punishment from the universe. I tried to refuse to take the part, but then Mum started asking all these questions about why, and suggested speaking to Miss Rotimi again. I had to make sure that didn't happen, so I agreed to do the stupid singing solo. Now I'm forced to spend time with the two people who are ruining my life: Lenny, who I'm furious with for busting up my friendship with Donna; and Miss Rotimi, who's busting up my parents' marriage.

Donna won't speak to me. Made all the easier because she's not been at school, and we break up for holidays today.

At home, Mum and Dad are frostier than

Frosty the snowman. Christmas is going to be icy.

'I *said*,' says Miss Rotimi, 'look into his eyes.'

I try to look into Lenny's eyes. They are dark brown, and deep and intense . . .

He cracks up.

I can't help it; I laugh too.

We're in another rehearsal at lunchtime. These ones are just for me and Lenny to get to grips with our duet. The concert is on Saturday so we only have three more days. Miss Rotimi is making us come in tomorrow and Friday as well, even though school has finished. I'd never have thought it was possible, but it's only one song and we're already off-sheet. Miss Rotimi has got us working on polishing our performance.

Miss Rotimi sighs. 'Concentrate please, you two.'

But every time I try to look at Lenny he pulls a silly face that Miss Rotimi can't see — flaring his nostrils and waggling his ears.

I roll my eyes. I'm not impressed.

'What?' says Lenny with a cheeky grin. 'Is there something funny about my face?' he asks, then he makes a weird grimace – scrunching up his mouth.

I scowl. But he does look quite funny.

'You're not helping!' Miss Rotimi snaps at him.

'He's not, is he?' I say.

'Control yourself,' she says. 'We can't have you being silly when you're onstage.'

My mouth snaps shut. The reality of the concert suddenly hits me.

'Oh God,' I mutter. 'I'm going to completely mess this up, aren't I?'

'With that attitude,' says Miss Rotimi, 'you just might.'

Singing this song in the concert is going to put me centre stage for about three minutes. Onstage, with the amazing adrenalin rush it brings. I used to hate being the centre of attention, but now, if I'm honest, I'm looking forward to that feeling. I'm going to be special for one brief moment. Lenny has helped me feel OK with feeling special.

'Right, start from the top,' says Miss Rotimi. 'I want you two to hold hands.'

I don't want to hold his hand. I might like it too much.

'Go on,' she says, motioning to our hands.

Lenny takes a deep breath and looks at me. His stare is still intense, but this time it's not so funny. He holds both my hands. I get a tingling feeling up my arm when he touches me. Even though I know I shouldn't, I really like how my skin feels against his. I hate myself.

'Good,' says Miss Rotimi. 'Then when you sing, *I really can't stay . . .*'

That's my line.

'You pull away from him,' she says.

'♫ *I really can't stay* ♫' I sing, and I wrench my hands out of his.

'No, no, no,' says Miss Rotimi. 'Not like that.' She gets up from behind the piano and comes over to us. 'Don't you understand the subtext of the song?'

'I don't even understand the word *subtext*,' I tell her.

Lenny laughs, which earns him a look from Miss Rotimi.

She shakes her head and thrusts my hands into Lenny's again.

'The woman is *saying* she can't stay,' Miss Rotimi explains, 'but she doesn't want to go. Not really. She *wants* to stay and kiss and cuddle with this gorgeous young man.'

I'm blushing. Why can't I control my body?

'Meanwhile,' she continues, 'he'll use any excuse to keep her here.'

'Even the weather,' adds Lenny.

'Exactly, Lenny,' she says. 'Very good.'

'But I don't think she *does* want to stay,' I say, sticking my chin up in the air. 'If she did, why wouldn't she just stay?' I know exactly how the girl in the song feels, but I'm determined not to give Lenny any mixed messages. I might like him, but he kissed me and kissed Donna and that makes him a pig.

Miss Rotimi shakes her head and smiles an annoying smug smile. 'Sometimes what we want is not something we can have.'

Is she talking about me? Or about my dad? I narrow my eyes at her.

'When we start again,' says Miss Rotimi, 'I

want to see all that conflict in your eyes. You want this man. But you know you shouldn't.'

I gulp. This is a little too close to the truth.

Miss Rotimi sits down behind the piano again. But then a phone beeps. She rummages in her bag to find it.

She beams as she looks at the screen, and jumps up again. 'Sorry, kids, I have to go. Emergency.' Her eyes have gone all twinkly and she's grinning like an award winner. 'We'll carry on after school, yeah?'

She doesn't wait for a response as she hurries from the room clutching her phone. I stare after her. Was the text from my dad? I wonder how I could find out. And what would I do if I did? Would I tell Mum?

'Want to carry on practising?' Lenny asks.

I walk away to get my bag. 'Nope,' I say. Even though part of me does.

He lurches forward and pulls me back. 'But it's cold outside.'

I squint at him. 'You're going to have to come up with something better than that. I'm not as stupid as the girl in the song.'

'The girl in the song isn't stupid,' he says. 'She's in love.'

That's a massive word. It makes us go silent.

'Come on,' he says. 'Just five more minutes.'

I glance at the door. Lenny has still got a hold of my hand and I'm afraid someone will see us. 'Sorry.' And I wrench out of his grasp just like Miss Rotimi told me not to. 'See you around.'

I walk away from him. And so he can't follow me, I go and hide in the girls' loos.

Donna still hates me. The other girls aren't blaming me, but that's only because they don't know what I've done. I didn't mean to get close to Lenny. But I did lie. A lot. I hung out with him in secret when I should have told Donna everything. And none of my deceitfulness was worth it, because he was stringing us both along.

All this time I've been angry with my dad for having an affair, when I've been doing the exact same thing. No matter how much I like Lenny, or how much we have in common, I should have stayed away from him. Like Dad should have stayed away from Miss Rotimi.

Now I have nothing – no Donna, no Lenny,

no orchestra, no Sucker Punch. Reece and Joel are really mad that the band is over, and they're blaming Donna. When actually everything is my fault.

And worst of all, I'm really missing hanging out with Lenny. Before I knew what he was really like, he was the only person I could talk to about my feelings, the only person I was honest with. I have so much going on in my head, trying to deal with all this drama, but the one person I want to speak to about it is the one person I can never speak to again. Because he's not the person I thought he was. I should never have listened to my stupid instincts. It's going to be the loneliest holidays ever.

I wasn't sure what this feeling was before, but now I know. My heart is breaking.

The door to the loos opens.

'*There* you are!'

It's Sonia. My face falls.

'I thought it must be you in here,' she says.

'What do you want?' I snap.

'Lenny's outside. He's waiting for you like a lost puppy.'

I sigh huffily. I can't blame her for being upset after what Donna did, but she's done nothing but stir things.

'What's up?' she asks.

'I don't have to tell you,' I say.

Sonia tilts her head to the side. 'You don't have to,' she says softly, 'but it looks like you need someone to talk to.'

She's totally got me there, and – oh God – I can feel my lip starting to wobble.

Sonia steps towards me and strokes my arm.

I want to back away, but I haven't really spoken to anyone in days. Not properly. And I really need a friend right now.

'Obi,' she says gently, 'what's the matter?'

Her kindness has turned the tap and suddenly I'm crying. She hugs me tightly.

'What's this all about?' she says, and she sounds like my mum when she's comforting me. Which only makes me cry harder. 'Lenny?'

'No!' I splutter quickly. I'm not stupid enough to trust Sonia again, but as soon as the words are out of my mouth I know they're another lie. I've got to stop doing this.

'Yes,' I say, deciding that it's time to tell the truth, even if Sonia does have a hidden agenda. I can't keep all these secrets any more.

Sonia has her chin resting on my shoulder and I can feel her nodding. 'Thought so,' she says.

What a mess.

'Have you broken up?' she asks.

I come out of the hug to look Sonia in the eye, so she knows I'm telling the truth. *Now* at least.

'We were never together,' I say. And I think about how he kissed Donna just after kissing me.

Sonia raises an eyebrow.

'Honestly!' I say. But although that may be the truth, it's not the *whole* truth.

'But he likes you,' she says. '*Really* likes you.'

Despite kissing Donna, I think he does.

I nod. 'Yes.'

He said he was comforting her — no doubt about her parents' break-up — when they were hugging at the party. But she said he kissed her. How can I know for sure that he likes me after that?

Sonia shakes her head. 'I'm not asking, I'm *telling* you: Lenny really likes you.'

Sonia used to be so sure that Lenny liked Donna — now she's telling me he likes me.

'How do you know?' I ask with a sniff. I hate myself for being curious after what he's done.

'Because he asked me to give you this,' she says. She opens her hand. Inside is a gold chain. And on the end of the chain is a pick. It's purple and blue, meshed together in a cloud design.

Lenny's lucky pick.

I gasp. Lenny wouldn't give that up for anyone. But he's given it to me.

'He told me you won't speak to him,' she says. 'I helped you two get together — swapping numbers, arranging music dates — so he thought he could trust me with this too.'

I shake my head. Lenny might trust her, but I don't. 'But why would he want me to have it?' I take the pick and look at it closely. I know how precious it is to him.

'Isn't it obvious?' she says. 'He's trying to prove how much he cares.' She lifts the pick from my hand and puts it round my neck like a medal. It's like I've won a competition. The prize is Lenny.

I look at the pick. If he's giving this to me, I must really mean a lot to him. Whatever's going on between him and Donna, he definitely likes me. No one has ever made me feel this special.

'Do you fancy him?' she asks me.

I think about it. I'm not being dishonest any more, but I just don't know the answer. Maybe there's some kind of explanation about why he kissed Donna. Could it be more complicated – just like he said?

'I don't know if I fancy him.' But as soon as I say it I realize that I *do* know. I've wanted to be Lenny's girlfriend this whole time. And as I'm not going to lie any more, I have to tell the truth.

'Actually,' I say, 'I do fancy him. I really do.'

There's no way I can have Lenny as a boyfriend and have Donna as a best friend. But that's what I want more than anything. And somehow this mess keeps getting worse.

Chapter 30

There's a knock on my door. I groan. Was that too much? Mum pokes her head round.

'Are you ready to . . . Oh! Obi!' she says. 'Are you OK?'

I shake my head. 'No,' I say. 'I don't feel well.'

This isn't a lie. My stomach's been churning all day. OK, I don't think I have bubonic plague or anything, but I definitely feel sick. Still, this is the new me and I'm not lying any more. About anything.

'I don't want to go,' I say.

It's Saturday night. I'm sitting on my bed, school uniform on, even though it's school holidays, about to head over to the concert. But although I may seem ready, I'm not. Not mentally.

'You look awful,' Mum says, her eyes filled

with concern. She comes over and puts a hand on my forehead. 'You don't feel hot.'

'I'm not ill,' I tell her. 'I just don't want to go.'

Mum smiles at me like I'm being foolish. 'It's natural to be nervous, honey, ask your father. But—'

I shake my head. 'It isn't stage fright,' I say.

The thought of being centre stage is definitely scary, but I want to sing at the concert so badly. I want to feel the crowd's eyes on me, and their applause as I do a good job. I want to feel special. Lenny's helped me to see that. But I can't go.

Mum looks even more worried now. She sits down next to me. 'So what's the matter?'

Where do I start?

'I haven't been going to the practices,' I say.

I've bunked them all since school finished on Wednesday.

'Why not?'

I sigh. 'I was supposed do them with that boy Lenny. But I don't want to see him.'

'Don't you like him?'

'No.'

Honesty, Obi, I remind myself.

'I mean, yes. I do. That's half the problem.'

Mum smiles again. 'You like him. And you don't know if he likes you back. Is that it?'

I shake my head. 'He *does* like me back. That's the other half of the problem.'

Mum's looking into my eyes and I realize this is the first proper chat we've had in ages. Maybe since I was in Year 3 and confessed to her about breaking a school ruler and putting it back without telling. She was so nice about that then, and she's being so nice now.

'He's told me he fancies me and wants to be my boyfriend. I fancy him too . . . but so does Donna. And Donna's my best friend . . . Or at least, she was.'

Mum leans back a little bit. 'Ah,' she says. 'That's a tricky one.' She bites her nail. 'There's no easy solution. But if you like him and he likes you then it shouldn't be an issue. If Donna's really your friend, she should be happy for you.'

'It's so hard at Hillcrest. I've been trying with my work and everything but—'

'I know you have, darling,' she says. 'And I

know I'm tough on you. But it's only because I care.'

I nod. 'I know.'

'Although I'm not thrilled about you missing practices, or having a boyfriend at your age, you're getting to that stage in life. I can't keep you as my baby forever.'

'But I don't want a boyfriend.' I think about Lenny's gorgeous smiley face, his ears wiggling to make me laugh. 'Well, maybe I do a little,' I admit. 'But mostly I want a best friend. I can't betray Donna. I refuse.'

Mum kisses me on the head. 'That's what I love about you, Obi. You're so loyal.'

Mum has no idea. I've been the most *dis*loyal, *dis*honest girl in the world.

'But you must sing tonight. You made a commitment to the school and to Miss Rotimi.'

I turn away when she says her name.

'She must have gone in especially for those practices,' Mum continues. 'Poor woman.'

I can't bear to lie to Mum, but I honestly don't know what's going on with Miss Rotimi and my dad. I don't think it should come from me.

'And *I* want to hear you sing,' she adds. 'I've not paid enough attention to your music before and it's high time I did.'

I sigh. There's no way out of it now.

'Will you get Dad for me, please?' I ask her.

Mum hesitates for a second, then nods. She leaves the room and I hear her calling for Dad. He thunders up the stairs and they talk outside my room.

'What's the . . .' Dad starts.

'Obi doesn't want to go tonight,' Mum whispers.

'But—'

'Talk to her.'

My heart starts racing. My family never speaks about stuff – not serious stuff anyway. But I just spoke to Mum about Lenny, and even though she didn't have any solutions, I think it helped. Now I'm going to speak to Dad about Miss Rotimi.

Dad walks in and he looks like Mum did: worried. I look back at him sternly, the way he used to look at me when he was about to tell me off.

His jaw clenches as he waits to hear what I'm about to say. 'What's up, Little Heart?'

I get up from the bed, crouch down and reach under it. My fingers touch the record. The one by Bobby Benson. The one that Miss Rotimi asked me to give to him. I pull it out, and when he sees what I'm holding he instantly recognizes it.

'Oh my! Is that . . . ?' He rushes over to me. 'Is this for me?' He pulls it from my hands and his face looks like Bem's did when he was given the Nintendo last Christmas. 'This record is impossible to find!' He says, flipping it over like he can't believe it's real. 'What a Christmas present! Where did you get it?' He carries on muttering about how he's been looking for this particular one for ages, how he thought it didn't exist on vinyl any more. This only shows just how much Miss Rotimi has been trying to impress him. I'm saying nothing, just glaring at Dad until finally he looks at me. I bite my lip. His face falls.

'Miss Rotimi gave it to me,' I tell him.

'How nice of her. But why would she give

283

you something so precious? This is something only a jazz lover . . .' He trails off. 'She gave it to *me*, didn't she?'

I nod. 'She gave it to me to give to you. But I didn't. Because there was a note inside saying she wanted to meet up with you.'

Dad sighs and sits down on the bed.

'Meet up with you *again*.'

He runs his hands over his head.

I have to ask him.

'Are you having an affair with her?'

My little heart is pounding. It makes me feel sick.

He shakes his head. 'No.'

I feel relieved. But only a bit. I don't know much about relationships, but Dad looks ashamed so I know there's something going on.

'But she wants to?' I ask.

He pauses. 'I don't know.'

I thought life was tough but then you left school and grew up, got married, had kids and things became easy. But it's not like that. No one's perfect. It turns out that adults can be stupid when it comes to relationships – just as stupid as us kids. And like Mum said, sometimes there isn't an easy solution.

'Did you show this to your mother?' Dad asks.

'No,' I say. 'But you need to sort it out. You need to tell Miss Rotimi to back off. She only asked me to be in the concert to get to you.'

All of my feelings about Lenny and Donna are mixed up with my feelings about my dad and Miss Rotimi. No wonder I'm such a mess.

Thing is, it was Lenny who told me I had to actually speak to my family. And he was right. It was Lenny who made me feel special enough to want to perform. I miss him so much – as a friend or a boyfriend, I don't know. It doesn't really matter. I just miss him. He said he had an explanation for what happened with Donna – maybe it's time to hear it. And if it's a good explanation then . . . who knows?

'I'll talk to her,' Dad says. 'Before the concert. Come on – let's go.'

Maybe tonight's the night where everything gets sorted.

*

I'm flanked by Mum and Dad. I'm carrying my trumpet, even though I'm not playing it tonight. But I need a trumpet in my hand like Lenny needs his pick. I have Lenny's pick on the chain around my neck.

The concert isn't due to start for another half-hour, but the school's already packed. Everyone is running around, looking stressed, tuning up their instruments and making sure they have their sheets of music in the right order.

'Have you all remembered to bring your music?' Miss Rotimi is standing at the front of the hall. She looks a little stressed too, a pencil sticking out of her hair. But she also looks gorgeous. Light make-up that matches her green and red dress. She's wearing baubles for earrings, and even though they look silly, they also look good. It's awful but it's true: Mum's pretty but this woman is prettier. I hope Dad is a big enough man to see past that.

She spots us walk in and smiles. But only at Dad.

'Tumo!' she says. 'You're here! For a minute I thought our star performer wasn't coming.'

Mum clears her throat. 'Hello, Miss Rotimi.'

Miss Rotimi looks rattled, but just for a second. 'Oh . . . hello . . . Mrs Udugo.' Then she plasters an even bigger smile on her face. 'I didn't think you'd come. Tumo says you've been working all hours of the day and night and hardly have time for anything else.'

The double meaning is clear – she's implying that Mum's been neglecting her family and also that she knows all this stuff about Dad.

'I wouldn't miss it for the world,' says Mum, fake-smiling her right back. 'And, please, call me Shannon.'

'Obi,' Miss Rotimi turns to me. 'We've missed you at rehearsals. I've had to take the song out of the show.'

'Put it back in,' I tell her. 'I'm ready.'

'Are you sure?' she asks, dropping an eyebrow because she's unconvinced.

I think about getting up onstage in front of everyone. It makes me scared, but also excited.

'The show must go on,' I growl at her.

Dad looks between the three women gathered

here. 'Ife,' he says to Miss Rotimi, 'can I have a quick word?'

Mum looks a little surprised and I wonder if it was wise for Dad to say it so blatantly like that. But she backs off. 'I think I see Tara's mum over there,' she says. 'I must say hello.'

Dad leads Miss Rotimi out of the hall and down the corridor. On one hand I don't want to hear what they have to say; on the other, I *need* to hear it. I find myself following them, hiding round the corner.

When I get there, Dad's saying, '. . . appreciate your friendship. There's been a lot of stuff going on at home and you've been really great to talk to.'

'You know I'd do anything for you,' she simpers.

I'm tempted to run around and whack her.

'But I love my wife,' Dad says. It makes me smile. 'I'm sorry if you thought otherwise.'

'Bu—' she starts. Once again a beautiful person can't believe she's being turned down.

'Nothing is ever going to happen between us,' he says.

I punch the air. This means that they haven't had an affair. As much as Miss evil Rotimi tried.

All this time I was worrying about something that never happened! My parents aren't splitting up, and I'm so relieved I could cry. I know I wouldn't be able to take it as well as Donna's taking her parents' divorce. My family is safe and my dad loves my mum. I'm so glad I spoke to him about it. Maybe Donna was partly right when she said you don't have to tell everyone everything. But Lenny was right too. For the big things, it's better to talk it through.

And there's someone I need to talk to right now.

Chapter 31

When I get back to the hall, there's no need to ask if the Boys' School Girls have arrived: they are the loudest thing in there – and that includes the tuning-up orchestra.

My dad's talked to Miss Rotimi and now that's all sorted. If I can just fix everything with Donna too, then tonight will be perfect. Lenny's lucky pick must be working.

'Hey, Obi,' says Tara, seeing me approach. 'Ready for your big solo?'

I beam. 'Kind of.' I wrinkle my nose. 'Nervous excitement, you know.' With what's just happened I'd forgotten that's why I'm here. But I'm feeling so positive that I could do anything, even sing an unrehearsed song, with a boy I fancy, in front of hundreds of people.

I find Donna. She's standing next to Candy and Indiana. Amazingly, she looks really good. I don't mean that meanly, but you'd think, with her parents breaking up, that she'd be suffering. Instead she looks even better than normal after her week off. She's wearing tight jeans and a cut off T-shirt and her cropped Converse. And although it shouldn't go, she's wearing an oversized scarf with it. Donna's dress sense is always spot on, even when it's a little off key.

I smile at her. She gives a half-smile back. 'Hi, Obi,' she says.

Half-smiling is a good start! Maybe she'll forgive me. Maybe she's been missing me as much as I've been missing her.

We look at each other shyly, totally aware that all eyes are on us. The girls know we haven't spoken all week. 'You look great,' I tell her.

She does a little curtsy and it makes me laugh.

'Shall we talk?' I say to her.

She nods.

We walk away from the others towards the girls' loos. I'm surprised that she's the one taking my arm, leading the way.

'How're things at home?'

She flaps her hand. 'Oh bleurgh!' she says. 'Mum won't stop crying. Dad's not been in touch at all, not even with me.'

'That's awful!' I say.

She shrugs. 'In a way. But Mum's so clueless I can stay up all night watching TV. Even though Dad hasn't called, he must be feeling guilty as he keeps putting money into my account. And the school's let me off everything. I don't have to do any homework over the holidays!'

She laughs but I'm wary of joining in. 'You're making it sound like it's a good thing your parents are divorcing.'

'Don't get me wrong,' she says. 'It sucks. All I'm saying is . . . it has its benefits too.'

'You're amazing,' I tell her. There's no way I'd be able to see the positive side if it was happening to me. Things must have been really bad at home.

'I try,' she says, curtsying again.

We get to the toilets and I take a deep breath. But I'm not as worried as I was earlier. I've got this talking thing nailed.

'So what's up?' she says.

My heart starts pounding again. So much for having it nailed.

'Umm . . .' I start. 'I miss you.'

Donna smiles – her real smile. 'I miss you too,' she says.

'I want to be friends again,' I say. 'But—'

'Oh! Me too!' she says, and she launches forward and gives me a hug. 'Is that why you're looking so nervous? Because you're afraid of being my friend?' She throws back her head and laughs. 'I was just being moody. But I'm back now.' She hugs me again.

I could leave it at that. But there are a few more things I need to say, even if she doesn't want to hear them.

'The thing is . . .' I squeak from her oxygen-constricting grip.

I have to tell her about Lenny. Whatever happens, she needs to hear it from me.

I hear a clatter of footsteps as the other girls bowl into the loos. I roll my eyes. 'Sorry, girls,' I say to them. 'Could Donna and I have another moment, please?'

They're about to back out of the door when

Sonia steps forward. 'Ahh, isn't this sweet?' she says. 'Best friends making up.'

Donna glares at her. 'So what if we are, Sonia?'

'Come on, Sonia,' says Abby. 'These two need to talk.' She grabs Sonia's arm, but Sonia isn't budging.

'I know they do.' She looks so smug. 'And I know what they need to talk about.'

'Sonia, please,' I say. 'This will be better coming from me.'

'You're right. When you've completely betrayed your *best friend*,' she makes air quotes with her fingers, 'it *is* better if she hears it from you.'

'Sonia . . .' But what can I say? This is where Sonia gets her revenge. With what Donna and I did to her, I should have guessed it was coming.

'Hears *what*?' says Donna with a sigh. 'One of you spill, will you? Obi's got her big moment onstage any second.'

I'm glad Donna's back to her old self. I should have known she wouldn't be dented for long. But if Sonia's about to do what I think, then all Donna's confidence will be shot down for good.

'It's about Lenny,' I say, quickly, before Sonia can do it. But I can't quite look at her. The words won't come out of my mouth.

Donna rolls her eyes, looking at the other girls like she wishes I'd get to the point. 'What about him?'

'He likes Obi,' says Sonia.

The other girls gasp.

'How do you know?' says Candy.

'We thought he liked Donna,' says Indiana.

'Likes Obi?' asks Abby. 'Or *like* likes Obi?'

'He *like* likes her,' says Sonia. '*Like* likes her a lot.'

I look at Donna but she's giving nothing away.

'And she *like* likes him back,' Sonia adds, eyes twinkling cruelly.

The girls gasp again.

'I . . .' I want to deny it but I've promised not to lie any more.

'They've been sending texts, sneaking round, meeting up in secret . . .' Sonia adds.

I put my head in my hands. We did meet up for secret practices. We do tell each other our secrets.

'Obi?' Donna turns to me.

I close my eyes. 'It's true.'

'And he gave her this,' says Sonia. My eyes are closed so I don't see her move, but suddenly I feel her hands on my neck. She pulls out the chain with the pick on it.

Tara gasps the loudest. 'Lenny's lucky pick!'

'Did he give that to you?' asks Candy.

'I . . .' I say again. Being honest is not so easy in front of a crowd. 'Yes,' I finally admit.

The room goes quiet, which never happens around all these girls. It feels like I could drown in the silence.

Everyone's looking at Donna. Her cheeks are pink. She must be hurt and humiliated at the same time.

'Obi,' she says, 'that's fantastic!'

What?!

'Huh?' says Sonia, behind me.

'What are you all looking at me like that for?' asks Donna, flipping her hair.

'Aren't you angry with me?' I ask, the words coming out with a stutter. Donna frowns as if I've just asked her to wear orange and yellow at the same time. 'Why would I be angry with you?'

There's another silence for a million years, and then . . . 'Because *you're* in love with Lenny!' Candy screeches.

I can't believe Candy's said it out loud, but that's what we were all thinking.

Donna frowns. 'What? Have you gone crazy?' Then she starts laughing and laughing. 'Oh my God, that's so funny! You all thought I'd be upset that my best friend has got herself her first boyfriend? What kind of person would that make me?'

That's kind of what my mum said.

Maybe the Girl Code is nonsense. Maybe, like my mum said, Donna is a good enough friend that she wants me to be happy. Even at the expense of her own happiness. 'You're not annoyed?'

Donna shrugs. 'Why would I be? I might have had a tiny crush on Lenny at one point.'

She swipes the air like she's swiping a screen. 'But not any more.'

I exhale with relief. This could turn out to be the best evening ever.

Sonia looks around at all of us, as if checking we're hearing what she's hearing. 'Er . . . since when?'

The look on Sonia's face is priceless. She's delivered her final blow and it's completely backfired. I understand she was desperately trying to get Donna back for ditching her, but she took it too far – and now it doesn't matter. Donna doesn't care about me and Lenny!

'Especially since . . .' Donna says, flipping her hair again and making sure all attention is on her, 'Darnell Wade started messaging me on Facebook.'

The girls gasp again, me included. This is a massive deal – Darnell's in Year 10. I assumed he didn't know any of us existed.

'How cool!' I screech. 'What did he say?'

Donna smiles a smug smile. 'Oh, you know, the usual stuff.'

But this kind of stuff never happens to me so I don't know what's usual and what's not.

'Tell me!' I say, pinching her on the arm.

'He said he liked my profile picture. He's seen me around school.'

'Has he asked you out?' I ask.

'He's in Year 10,' she says. 'He's hardly going to directly ask me, is he?'

'Of course not,' says Hannah. 'Year 10 boys are so much more sophisticated than that.'

'Exactly,' says Donna. Then she turns to me, cringing a little. 'Sorry. No offence, Obi. Lenny's great . . . as Year 8 boys go. It's just—'

'It's fine!' I say, beaming from ear to ear. And I'm not offended at all.

Donna doesn't want to go out with Lenny any more. And if my instincts are right, and Lenny isn't the bad guy that he seems, he's a free man. This means I can go out with him and still be friends with her and keep to the Girl Code.

Just wait till I tell Lenny.

Chapter 32

The orchestra plays the last few notes of *Oh, Christmas Tree* while I look on from behind the curtain. They've been practising hard and they sound so good. It's not quite big band, but it's close. I wish I was with them, taking my place in the brass section and blasting out the notes.

Miss Rotimi is in the front, conducting. I'm so happy right now I don't even hate her that much any more. By the end of this term she'll be gone, off to pester the married men at some other new school, I bet. My dad's told her to bug off. Mum and Dad are sitting next to each other in the audience. They aren't holding hands or anything, but they look happy to be here and I see them smile when they catch each other's eye.

'You ready?' whispers Lenny beside me.

I smile up at him. 'I'm a bit nervous,' I say.

And I am, but not just about that. Now that I know Donna doesn't fancy him, I plan to speak to him after the concert. I want to hear his explanation at last. And if it's a good one, I'm going to tell him I want to be his girlfriend after all.

'You?' I whisper back.

He nods. 'Especially as we haven't practised at all.'

I cringe.

'You made me come into school in the holidays,' he says. He's smiling but he must have been annoyed. 'For nothing!'

'Yeah, sorry about that.' I look him in the eye. 'I'll make it up to you.'

Lenny beams.

Suddenly the *nervous* overtakes the *excitement* and a wave of terror shoots through me.

'I have to pee!' I say.

Lenny pulls a face like he's disgusted. 'Knock yourself out.'

I turn and run. As soon as I'm out of the door, I jump down the last steps and sprint to the loo. The fittest boy in school – apart from

Darnell Wade – wants to go out with me. For the first time in my life, I know I'm special. At least, I'm special to Lenny.

I push the doors to the loo and run inside a cubicle. I'm just about to sit on the loo when I hear something that makes me stop.

Gulping and sniffing. Someone's crying.

'Hello?' I say.

The noises stop.

'Is anyone there?' I ask.

Silence.

I open the door and come out of the cubicle. Getting down on my hands and knees, I check underneath the stall with the closed door. Cropped Converse.

'Donna?'

The shoes don't move.

'Donna,' I say. 'I can see you.'

Still she says nothing.

But I'm not going to let her be miserable by herself. 'I'm coming in.'

Slithering along the floor, I crawl into her cubicle. It's cramped in here with the door locked, but I just manage to get up. Donna's face is blotchy and red. She looks terrible, mascara all down her cheeks.

I've never seen her look like this: imperfect.

'Donna!' I say. 'What's wrong?'

She starts sobbing again. I hug her, something I never thought I'd ever be good at, but since joining this school I've learned to hug. Girls hug a lot.

'What's wrong?' I ask again. 'You were so happy a few minutes ago.'

She shakes her head.

'Has something else happened with your mum and dad?' I ask. 'Or is it Darnell?'

Donna cries harder. 'It's a little bit to do with my mum and dad,' she sniffs, 'but nothing to do with Darnell.'

'Oh.'

'It's nothing to do with Darnel . . . because I made all that up,' she says.

'Oh,' I say again. 'So what is it?'

'My best friend is seeing the boy I like,' she says. 'And she's been doing it behind my back!'

My cheeks burn. I feel awful. I should have known she wasn't OK with it. Donna told me not to tell everyone everything. And while I thought *she* told everyone everything, only now am I realizing she doesn't say a word about herself. Not the stuff she really cares about. Not about how she feels.

'I'm sorry, Donna,' I say. 'I've been a complete cow.'

'No less than I deserve,' she says. 'I'm a complete cow to everyone. Finally, it seems, it's payback time.'

'What do you mean?'

'Not getting the part in the concert,' she says. 'You and Lenny. My parents divorcing. All of this is because I'm a terrible person.'

I grab her hand and squeeze it tight. 'You are *not* a terrible person.'

'Then why is this happening to me?' she asks. 'I can't take much more.'

I don't have an answer for that. 'Because life sucks sometimes. I know it probably doesn't help,' I go on, 'but I didn't mean for this stuff with Lenny to happen. It just did.'

Donna exhales heavily. 'That's the way relationships *should* start. I've been trying so hard to get him to fall for me. Thinking of ways to be alone with him. Making him hot chocolate, and finding excuses to touch him.'

So Lenny didn't touch her – she touched him.

'But if I have to try so hard, then he doesn't like me,' she says. 'With you, you didn't want it to happen, but it happened anyway.'

I never thought he would like me so I never tried to impress him. He fell for the real me.

'I don't understand,' I say. 'Why would he like me when he could have you?'

'Your natural beauty,' says Donna.

I splutter. 'Give me a break! No one would ever call this hair all over the place, these short legs and this skinniness *beautiful*. I make stupid jokes. I'm feisty. I say the wrong thing at the wrong time. I have no idea *what* to say.'

'What you see is what you get with you,' she says. 'That's what Lenny likes. You don't even have to try.'

I don't try because I know I could never succeed. Not in being as beautiful as someone like Donna.

'I try so hard,' she says, gulping a little, 'but I'll never be good enough. Not for Lenny. Not even for my dad. And he's supposed to love me unconditionally.'

'I'm sure your dad loves you,' I say to her.

'Oh yeah?' she snaps back. 'Then why has he left me and my mum? Why, even before that, was he never at home? He buys me loads of stuff. But he never wants to spend time with me.'

I've never met her dad so I don't know what's going on there. I'm guessing it's more to do with Donna's mum than Donna. Because who wouldn't want to spend time with Donna – she's awesome!

'It's his loss,' I tell her.

'Pah!' she splutters.

Seeing her like this makes me want to make it all better for her. I hate that I've hurt her. Of course she still likes Lenny – she's liked him for so long, and that's not going to just go away. And of course she made up that stuff about Darnell Wade. She did it to make us think she was OK when she's anything but.

Donna's confidence is just an act; I see that

now. Like my dad said about getting onstage and faking it. That's what Donna does every day.

'I've lied a lot to you too,' she says. 'I never kissed Lenny.'

I can't help it, I smile. It's the explanation I've been waiting for! They never kissed. He's not a pig.

'You should go out with him,' she says.

'What?! No,' I say. 'I would never—'

Donna holds up her hand. 'You two clearly like each other. And even though I was lying about Darnell when we were with the other girls earlier, I wasn't lying when I said you're my best friend. And as your best friend, I should be happy for you.'

'Donna . . .' It was Sonia who first mentioned the Girl Code, and she might be mean, but she does know more about friendship than I do.

'Please,' says Donna. 'I won't be upset if you go out with Lenny. I promise.'

That's what best friends do for each other. And if she's giving up Lenny for me, then there's a gift I have to give up for her.

'OK,' I say. 'First, I'm going to get you out

of this cubicle.' I unlock the door and suck in so I can open it around us both. 'It's no good for your singing voice.'

Donna frowns, confused.

'Second,' I say, taking her hand and pulling her out towards the mirror, 'I'm going to clean up the make-up that's all down your face.'

Donna's eyes go wide at the thought of what she looks like right now.

'I'm no expert,' I say to her, 'but I don't think big black streaks have ever been a feature in *Hot or Not.*'

Donna looks in the mirror and gives an exaggerated gasp when she sees her reflection. 'Not!' she yelps.

I take off my school jumper, wet the sleeve under the tap and give it to her to wipe her face.

'But I don't have my make-up bag with me,' she says. 'I can't reapply.'

'Good,' I say. 'Because you're not going to reapply.'

'Are you crazy?!' she squeals. 'The world is not ready. There isn't a Circle of Shame big enough to cover my whole face.'

I take my wet jumper from her and dab away the last streaks of make-up. 'You're beautiful, Donna. Inside and out. You might not be perfect, but there's a boy out there somewhere who will think you are.' I remember Lenny telling me I was perfect. 'And it won't have anything to do with how you look.'

Donna bites her lip but allows me to wipe away the rest of her make-up.

Her face is red. Her eyes aren't prettied up with mascara and eyeliner. They're a little puffy and her face is a little blotchy. But she still looks beautiful.

Just then, the toilet door bursts open. Tara, Abby and Maxie barge in.

'Oh my God, Obi!' says Tara. 'What are you doing here? Miss Rotimi is going nuts.'

I smile at the idea of Miss Rotimi worrying. Let her.

'She sent us to look for you,' says Maxie. 'It's time for your solo.'

'I'm not doing my solo,' I tell them. There's someone who deserves it so much more than me.

The girls look worried.

'But . . .' says Abby. 'What do we tell Miss Rotimi?'

'Tell her: the show must go on,' I say.

Donna suddenly catches on to what I'm suggesting. 'No way.' She holds her hands up. 'I'm not going out there. Not like this.'

'You know the song,' I remind her. 'Let your natural beauty and your stunning voice blind them.'

'You're mad,' she says.

'Come on,' I say, leading her out of the loos. 'Do it for me. I never wanted to be in the concert anyway.'

I promised I wouldn't lie again, but I just told one more. I *did* want to be in the concert. I wanted to play the trumpet and sing a solo in front of everyone – particularly my parents – and show everyone I'm as special as anyone else.

But that was the last lie I'll tell. And I'll do it for Donna.

Chapter 33

Donna and I are arm in arm as we show up backstage. She took quite a lot of persuading, pestering and promises of no posting photos to get her here, but she's here. And I'm not lying when I say she looks beautiful without her make-up on.

Miss Rotimi's eyes widen when she sees me. 'Where have you been?' she asks. 'We had to push back the solo to after *We Three Kings*. You've messed up the running order!'

Messing things up is normally Miss Rotimi's job. 'I'm here now.'

She shakes her head. 'Right,' she says. 'I'll go on and introduce you both. Lenny? Are you ready?'

Lenny appears by my side. He nods. 'I think so.'

The orchestra finishes the final bars of *We*

Three Kings and Miss Rotimi walks out, joining in with the round of applause that's erupted across the school hall.

'Thank you again to the Hillcrest High orchestra,' she says. The applause dies down and everyone goes quiet. 'But now we have something a little special. A singing duet from two pupils in Year 8.'

From my spot in the wings, I can see my mum and dad straighten up in their chairs.

'This is us,' says Lenny.

I shake my head at him.

He looks confused. 'What?'

Miss Rotimi says, 'May I present, Lenny Fulton and Obi Udogu!'

More applause.

'Go on,' I tell him and give him a smile to say good luck . . . and sorry.

Of course he doesn't understand my smile, and he shrugs as he walks out on to the stage. He turns to the crowd and waves, picking out his mum in the crowd.

'Break a leg,' I say, and give Donna a hug.

'Thanks, Obi,' she says.

Donna takes a deep breath and steps out. She waves at the crowd and some people – people who know Donna and know she's not called Obi – look confused. My parents look most confused of all. I hope they aren't too disappointed. But I had to do this for my friend.

Miss Rotimi is furious. Which isn't why I'm doing this, but it is an added bonus.

Lenny looks at Donna. He smiles at her like an old friend, then realizes it's not who it's supposed to be. Then he looks back at me, still standing in the wings.

I shake my head at him again.

The orchestra starts up, playing the first notes of *Baby, It's Cold Outside*.

Donna takes the mic, smiles at Lenny and steps forward.

She starts to sing and it's amazing. I know she's nervous, standing in front of everyone with no make-up on, but her natural beauty is her singing ability. She hits every note perfectly, and when her voice mingles with the brassy big band of the orchestra, it gives me the tingling

313

feeling that I only normally get when I listen to the greats. I wish it was me up there — but hearing it done so well is the next best thing.

Lenny falters, opening his mouth and closing it, before finally getting his line out.

When Donna sings, she's looking up at Lenny.

But Lenny is still looking at me in the wings. '♫ *Been . . . hoping . . . drop . . .* ♫' He's fumbling his words.

Donna closes her eyes and turns to the crowd. She does her line as if nothing's wrong.

Lenny stops singing but Donna picks up his part.

As she sings that his hands are like ice, she steps forward and takes his hands. This is what Lenny and I had practised with Miss Rotimi. Donna wasn't there but somehow she knows what to do. It's instinctive for her.

Lenny misses his line. He drops Donna's hands and starts walking off the stage. Towards me.

Oh God. This is all going to backfire. Donna is left on her own. Miss Rotimi panics, looking at Lenny walking away from his mic. But Lenny's eyes are set on mine.

Donna calls after him, still in character. You'd have to know Donna as well as I do to know she's freaking out a little – just a slight drop in her jaw and a crinkle on her forehead. But I see it.

Some of the audience chuckle. Despite her nerves, Donna manages to style it out and carries on singing.

Lenny reaches me. 'Why aren't you out there?'

'Lenny!' I whisper. 'Get back onstage.'

'Not until you come with me,' he says.

I clamp my mouth shut.

'At least talk to me.' He dips his head down so he's looking me in the eye.

'Please, Lenny,' I say, leaning round to see past him. 'Don't leave Donna singing on her own.'

But Donna has taken centre stage. She's standing in front of the audience, beaming.

'♫ *He really couldn't stay!* ♫' She gestures towards the wings, making a joke about Lenny walking off. The audience laughs again. Then Donna raises both her arms, asking everyone to join in.

The audience call out the chorus back at her. Even my mum and dad are singing along.

Donna beams and turns to the orchestra for their musical interlude before the next verse.

'You see,' says Lenny. 'She's fine.'

And I can't disagree. Donna was always supposed to be on that stage, doing what she's doing. It makes me so glad that I gave her my part. When Lenny takes my hand and leads me out of the hall, I let him.

We find the first empty classroom and head in there. I turn on the lights.

'I can't believe you just walked out in the middle of your performance,' I say to him with a smile, trying to lighten his intense mood.

Lenny's not smiling though. I can't look at him when he's being like this. He looks so sad

316

and so very handsome. My heart is squeezing and I'm having trouble breathing.

'You were right. I was a coward,' he says to me. 'I should have told Donna I didn't like her like that. I don't know why I didn't.'

If he'd told her from the beginning, then she would have never liked him that way for so long.

'And I should have explained to you why Donna and I were so close. She's just been having a hard time, with her parents splitting and everything.' He looks me in the eye. 'That's why I was giving her a hug at the party. I couldn't tell you because their divorce was her secret.'

He only meant to be a good friend to Donna. But he ended up leading her on. It's a relief to finally get the explanation I was looking for, and to know that my instincts about him were right.

'I'm sorry for messing it up, Obi,' he says. 'I never liked Donna. Not like that. I really, genuinely, totally like you.'

I believe him. It's not that I think I'm perfect or special or beautiful. But for some reason, Lenny thinks all those things.

'I know you do,' I say.

It's a relief to know he's the guy I always thought he was . . . but maybe that's not enough.

'So you'll go out with me?' he asks, his face full of hope. 'You'll be my girlfriend?'

I'm tempted to say yes. He's so nice. He's really been there for me these last few weeks. He gave me his prize possession to show how much he cares. I have to give it back.

I reach under the collar of my shirt and pull out Lenny's chain. 'I'm . . .'

But I stop speaking when I see the look on his face change.

'Where did you get that from?' he asks.

'I . . .' But then I realize what's happened. 'You didn't ask Sonia to give me this?'

'No,' he says. 'It went missing from the rehearsal room that day you ran out on me. Oh, I'm so pleased you found it!'

He holds out his hand, waiting for me to give the pick back. 'Thanks, Obi!' he says, beaming. 'Where *did* you find it?'

Sonia was stirring again. She must have stolen this from Lenny, then given it to me, so I would think he liked me loads, and so she could upset Donna.

'I would tell you, but then I'd have to kill you,' I say with a grin.

I'll speak to Sonia later. I'll apologize about the whole situation again, but also make her promise to stop her mean tricks. Right now, I've got to say something to Lenny and it's going to hurt us both.

'I do like you, Lenny,' I tell him. 'A lot. But I don't want to be your girlfriend.'

'Huh?'

'I know you didn't mean to hurt Donna, but you did.'

Lenny looks at the floor.

'My friendship with Donna is pretty new, but it's more important to me than being your girlfriend.'

'But—'

I shake my head at him. 'It's not going to happen.'

Lenny sighs and it comes out a little shaky.

'But I would like to be your friend,' I say, taking both his hands. 'If you want that.'

Lenny doesn't move. I wiggle his wrists around to try to make him smile, but it doesn't work.

Still looking at the floor, he says, 'Best friend.'

I gasp, then try to hide it, but I smile to myself. I have another good, close friend. His *best friend*. It didn't feel forced or too early or weird like it did when Donna first said it. And when I think about it, it's not even really a surprise. It just happened. Naturally. Like Donna said it would.

I give him a hug.

'Best friends . . . and band mates?' he asks. 'Will you persuade Donna to get Sucker Punch to re-form? And then, will you join us?'

I think it will be pretty easy to get Donna to get the band back together. She never really wanted them to quit in the first place. And if she's my friend, then she'll forgive me and the band will be back on. And even better, I'll be in it.

'If she ever agrees to speak to you again after you walked off stage just now, I'm sure she can be persuaded.'

I've finally got the best friend I've always wanted. Someone who is there for me and who I can trust with my secrets.

Who would have thought it would be a boy?

Chapter 34

The audience are all piling out of the school hall. I look around for my mum and dad. When they come through the doors, they're easy to spot because they're the only ones not smiling.

'Mum! Dad!' I call. A couple of other people look around as well – not surprising as most of the adults here answer to *Mum* and *Dad* too.

'Obi!' says Dad, looking worried. 'What happened? Why didn't you sing your solo?'

'Umm,' I say. 'Long story.'

Mum comes over and takes me by the shoulders. 'Are you OK?'

I nod. 'I'm fine. I just . . . Donna . . .'

Mum tilts her head to one side.

'She did a great job, didn't she?' I finish.

Mum nods – she gets it – but Dad still doesn't have a clue.

'After all this drama,' Mum says, 'I think we deserve a treat.'

'Good idea,' says Dad.

I look at Dad. 'Erm . . .' I want a word with mum on my own, but I can't tell him that.

Mum gives me a knowing look. 'Tumo,' she says, 'I think our girlie needs a girlie chat. Would you mind leaving us for a sec?'

'Not at all!' he says. 'I'll go speak to the brass players. One of those kids had an impressive embouchure – very mature.'

'Thanks, Dad,' I say. And just to show him there are no hard feelings, I give him a hug. 'I love you.'

He kisses me on the top of my head. 'Love you too, Little Heart.' Then he looks up at Mum. 'Both of you.'

Dad walks back towards the hall, dodging the mums and dads coming out. I see Miss Rotimi at the top of the stairs. She's watching Dad go but he doesn't even look at her. This makes me smile. I have no worries about them any more.

Mum pulls me away from the crowd and we stand in the corridor.

'Mum . . .' I start, but I don't know what to say.

'That was really nice of you,' she says filling in the silence I've left, 'to give Donna your part.'

'Hmm,' I say.

'I understand now,' she says. 'I realize what music means to you. And I know what a big deal tonight was. Which makes it all the more impressive that you gave it away. I wanted to hear you perform,' she says. 'But seeing you behaving like such a nice, kind girl makes me the proudest mother in the world.'

'Thanks, Mum.' It feels good to have someone appreciate how hard this evening was. And even better that it's my mum.

'I was being the most unsupportive parent that's ever walked the earth.' I see her eyes are filling. 'I've been so obsessed with my work that I've been stifling your dream. But next term you can do a little more music. We'll do whatever it takes to get you to lessons again.'

'And what if I wanted to join that band? Sucker Punch?'

Mum nods. 'Absolutely . . .' But she can't

help herself and she frowns. 'As long as your schoolwork doesn't suffer.'

I realize that it doesn't matter that Mum and I look different. She's my mum and she loves me – she might be strict about certain stuff, but that's because she cares. This is the best prize I could get tonight. My mum supporting me in my music means so much to me. And even if I never make it big or manage to make a career out of it, at least the lying will be over.

I've been harsh on Mum recently. Maybe we all have. She's been working really hard and instead of helping, we've been resenting it. But actually, it's been hardest for her. It's *us* who have been unsupportive.

'Is everything OK, really?' she bends down to look me in the eye.

I nod. 'I just . . .' But I'm thinking. I accused Lenny of leading Donna on, but maybe I led Lenny on too. 'Do you think people do stupid things just for their ego?' I ask Mum.

'Like what?'

'I don't know,' I say. 'Like hanging around

with someone you know you shouldn't because it makes you feel good.'

Mum sighs. 'No one's perfect, Obi. It's not just your father. But he's a—'

Argh! Mum thinks I'm talking about Dad when actually I was talking about me. 'Oh no. I didn't mean—'

'He's got a heck of an ego,' she says. 'And I'm sure he enjoys being friends with beautiful young ladies like Miss Rotimi. Ladies who get his jokes and can talk jazz with him.'

So Mum knew about Miss Rotimi all the time.

'Your dad is allowed to have female friends,' she says, looking at me seriously. 'I trust him. So should you.'

Now I feel bad. I automatically assumed Dad was having an affair. When actually, I was the one kind of doing that. Mum's right. I've no reason not to trust Dad. He's always been there for me.

'So you and Dad are OK?' I ask.

'We're fine,' she says. Then she sighs. 'Who am I kidding? You've seen us recently!' She

326

tries to turn it into a laugh but it's not very convincing. 'We've been having a tough time because I've been working so hard. But this stage of my project will be done next week. And guess what?'

'What?'

'Your father got me a Christmas present.'

'Really? Already?' This is a surprise. 'But Dad's always been a lastminute.com kind of guy.'

Mum laughs, genuinely this time. 'You've got it in one! He's got me and him a little holiday – lastminute.com!'

Now I laugh too. But then I pull a sad face. 'Just you two?'

Mum nods. 'Afraid so. I know you three probably want a holiday too, but I think your father and I need—'

'It's not that,' I say. 'It's that I know you're going to tell me Jumoke's in charge. He's going to be a nightmare!'

Mum laughs and she puts her arm around me. We walk back into the hall to drag Dad away before he freaks out the trumpet player with all his questions.

I started the night with nothing – a broken family, no Donna, no Lenny, and no band to play music with.

But I've ended the night with everything I wanted – my parents getting on, a kick-ass band, and two really good friends. And really, that's the most important thing. Because – just as we'll be supporting Donna through the next few really tough months while her parents divorce – a good friend will always be there for you. Now I have two, I can handle anything.

For special offers,
chapter samplers,
competitions
and more,
visit . . .

www.quercusbooks.co.uk
@quercuskids